EMOTO'S PROMISE

DROWNED EARTH

Eight novellas.
Eight Australian authors.
One watery apocalypse.

Scientists said that it would take 5000 years for Earth's
oceans to rise.

They were wrong.

After an asteroid collides with Antarctica, a tsunami
devastates the world's coastal cities and escalates the melting
of the ice caps.

These eight novellas set in various locations around Australia
explore the potential consequences of such a catastrophe.
They can be read in any order.

Prequel short story: Shards of Silver by Alanah Andrews
The Rise by Sue-Ellen Pashley
Fire Over Troubled Water by Nick Marone
Submerged City by Austin P. Sheehan
Tides of War by Marcus Turner
The Jindabyne Secret by Jo Hart
River of Diamonds by S. M. Isaac
Emoto's Promise by Shel Calopa
Salvaged by C.A. Clark

EMOTO'S PROMISE

SHEL CALOPA

DROWNED EARTH

First published by Deadset Press in 2020

www.aussiespeculativefiction.com

ISBN: 978-0-6487973-0-2

Cover design Copyright © Alanah Andrews

Edited by Alanah Andrews

www.aussiespeculativefiction.com

DEDICATION

For Heidi, never forget that different is gold.

CHAPTER ONE: INCOMPATIBLE

Macie lowered herself off the scorching gutter that trimmed the Reclamation Centre and rubbed her scalded hands. She had taken care to land quietly; pressing her back up against the sun-drenched building, commanding herself not to breathe, but knowing it would only postpone the inevitable. They would find her eventually. They always did.

For six years, the motes in DarwinTwo City had tailed Macie everywhere. The small charcoal boxes appeared seconds after her feet hit the city streets, like silent electronic rats scavenging through the dust for human crumbs. They swept voraciously behind her as if to erase all traces of her *incompatible* DNA, lest it contaminate their precious high-tech citadel.

She wouldn't be surprised if Mayor Wolfram himself was using them to monitor her movements, ensuring she spent every waking hour managing the ocean wall that encircled the city. Earning *her* life by keeping *his* kind safe from the treacherous waters beyond.

Not that there was much else to do, anyway. The whole beige city was made up of numans who rarely registered her presence.

Numans—huh! That was one of Wolfram's ideas too.

He had them all so tightly meshed with their AI symbiotes and gilded virtual worlds, that they had renamed themselves 'new humans' or numans as Wolfram liked to call them—unlike Macie, who was merely human.

It hadn't always been like that. When she was a child, there were a few others like her, normals who couldn't adapt to new tech. Ordinary people who smiled. Kids who splashed in puddles, invented nicknames, had sleepovers and played tag through the rooftop hydroponics lanes.

But as the years passed and automation increased, the city's need for normals diminished along with food allocations. One by one by one, they had disappeared—

until eventually it was just Wall Manager Macie, the numans and the motes.

A click from a steel door a metre away drew her attention. Macie let out a low slow whistle she hoped would be mistaken for an ocean breeze squeezing between the tall, tightly spaced buildings. It was a copy of the whistle that had wafted under her bedroom door earlier that morning.

Signal apparently received, the door opened and out shuffled her grandmother, Vala.

"Forgot ... your din-ner. Second time ... since ... Upgrade 24," she said in stilted syllables, as though she had forgotten how her jaw worked.

Vala's hair was pulled back into a severe bun and she wore the same dreary overalls as the rest of the numans. Her clothes hung from her thin frame like wet linen draped over a wire hanger, all pale from being left too long in the sun.

Vala had been pretty once, when she was human. Macie had seen her in old holopics; relaxing at a dinner table, crinkled hair flowing over her shoulders, eyes twinkling at someone off camera. Now Vala's face had drained to numan grey and her once calming blue eyes had settled into milky stone.

Macie wanted so desperately to hug Vala for the great risk she was taking, but she knew better. Physical contact would leave DNA traces on her grandmother—unexpected for that time of day—that would mark Vala as deviating from her workplan. Non-compliance was the greatest of crimes in DarwinTwo. It would likely result in a painful reboot to end Vala's recognition of her granddaughter.

Instead, Macie took the offered dinner pail and nodded her respect.

"Thanks, Gran," she whispered.

Half a flinch from her left eye was all the response Vala gave, before shuffling back inside and closing the door.

Remembering the shortness of time—no motes yet, but soon—Macie put the handle of the pail between her teeth, crouched to the ground and leapt back up to clasp the guttering. Then, moving hand over fist, she shimmied along the edge until she was around the corner of the building where a wide overhang made for a perfect escape platform. Once she hoisted herself up, it was an easy mote-free jog across the low roofs of the industrial sector.

When Macie arrived at a thoroughfare which led to the wall, she dropped back onto the pavement. Right on cue, two motes sped out of an adjoining alleyway and began their cleaning task.

"Gee, can't a girl take a dinner stroll," she said,

waving her pail at them in an exaggerated fashion. One of them shoved at her ankle, delivering a little spark of electricity from its outer casing that made her jump backwards, almost standing on the other mote.

"All right, all right, I'm going." Physical contact was unusual. This one must have new programming—she would have to watch for that in the future.

Only when Macie arrived back at the wall and climbed the rusty ladder to the top, did they finally leave. With a salute to the scurrying motes, she turned her back on DarwinTwo's towers with all their monotonous precision and sat down to gaze at the choppy sea.

She knew she ought to be afraid, like the numans. The first few floors of the city sat well below water level. If there was a breach of the old stone wall, it would be just as deadly for her organic form as for the technologically-augmented numans, yet the glistening blue waves always calmed her.

She squinted at the darkening horizon and wondered, not for the first time, if there was another girl sitting alone on another sea wall, somewhere across the ocean. Possibly a technologically *incompatible* girl like her.

A small swell hit the wall, sending a spritz of cool water up to her toes—the smell of salty brine pulling her back to the job at hand. The motes would expect her to walk the evening perimeter check soon, yet the closed dinner pail was still in her lap. It was time to finish her grandmother's mission.

Macie unlatched the clip on the side of the pail and opened the lid. It made her instantly queasy to see the clear plastic bag inside; its dusty contents telling an old story she had heard too many times before.

As she read the label attached to the bag, tears welled in her eyes.

Emily Banks, terminated at 9 months of age. Designation: ***incompatible DNA.***

Macie opened the little bag, said an old prayer for the dead she remembered from Vala long ago, and scattered Baby Emily's ashes into the water.

CHAPTER TWO: MISSING

It took Macie three days to allow herself to admit that something had gone terribly wrong after Emily's burial at sea.

Just like every other evening, she had ended that first day with a verbal report to the closest mote who, she assumed, had filed the report where all records ended up; Central Library.

As usual, there was not much to report: No breaches in the monstrous bluestone wall, not even a trickle. The ancient engineers had incorporated a robust polymer resin into the grouting between the stones to ensure it could withstand the pounding sea—even during high tides when the ocean rose up to greet the moon while wind blew in from the north-east.

Macie knew this because she was the sole Wall Manager. It was her job alone to repair the great wall. No numan would lower themselves to do manual labour alongside the terrifying ocean.

When Vala didn't return home to their apartment that first day, Macie had assumed that she was pulling an all-nighter at the Reclamation Centre. It happened sometimes. Mayor Wolfram would suggest a new growth reduction strategy to address a budget shortfall. The city senate would unanimously agree—they always did—and suddenly the Reclamation Centre would be busy around the clock, processing redundant numans.

On those days, if she looked across town from the south end of the wall, she could sometimes make out a slight glimmer in the air as heat rose from the Centre's furnaces.

**

The second day was excruciatingly boring—not a hint of a problem to report or repair. Macie's only choices were to gaze at the mirror-like sea she couldn't sail, or lap the monochrome city she couldn't leave. Even the clouds were dull. A uniform blanket of white stratus stretched across the sky from one horizon to the other.

She took her lunch break on the eastern arc of

the wall. There, she could at least see a hint of life beyond the big glass windows of the food production garden. The only place she knew that still had live plants.

It was twenty minutes of heaven, eating her vac-sealed protein composites while imagining the real vegies she might touch if she was ever given the garden tour she had been promised the day she was appointed as Wall Manager.

When she lodged her report that night, she felt compelled—in the interest of breaking the monotony—to include the three rare sprays of water that had leapt up to spritz her shins.

The report-receiving mote rewarded her initiative with a minor electric shock to her ankle and an order to re-check the wall. Twice.

It was a surly response. She wondered whether Wolfram might be watching her in real-time, through the mote's unblinking lens eye.

The extra checks caused Macie to arrive home late. The apartment was quiet. The pantry was empty. She assumed Vala had eaten and gone to bed early.

***

On the third day, there was a leak at adjunct JK-97. It wasn't much, only a trail of persistent water droplets sliding over the stones, but the location was an issue. The adjuncts were the weakest points in the wall. They were the places where there had once been attachments to the ancient structure; armaments, jetties, catchment nets and lookout towers. Remnants of a time when the waters were still rising and desperate climate refugees had made unsuccessful attempts to enter the last great city.

At JK-97, the only sign of the violent history was a series of seven brass rings inlaid deep into the stone. Every time she lapped that part of the wall, Macie would stop to run her fingers over the brass, wondering at their significance. What had been attached to the rings? Seven vessels? Seven steps up the wall for hurried soldiers?

That was exactly what she was doing when she noticed the leak. The join in the stones beneath the middle ring had degraded enough to allow the damp to seep through. Macie leaned in for a closer inspection.

As she watched, a tiny shard half the size of her smallest fingernail sheared off the stone and traced a path down the wall, riding the droplets that were fast turning into a trickle. She knew it wouldn't take much time for the trail to expand into a stream of trouble.

Macie needed to get the grout formula quickly, only she was at the furthest point from her workshop which adjoined the wall on the other side of the city. If she followed the looping sea wall, it would take half an hour each way. Including formulation and application, this would leave the leak unfixed for at least ninety minutes.

As much the thought of moving through numan territory unnerved her, she knew she would have to take the short route through the city centre. She squatted down and waved to gain the attention of the nearest mote. It scurried over and swivelled its big black eye up to her.

"Urgent report. Class 6 leak at JK-97. Leaving post to retrieve grouting. Taking direct route through city. Estimated fix time: fifty minutes. Wall Manager Macie out."

She shouldered her work bag and took off at a slow run, humming her navigation ditty as she moved. "Jade rowed a straight path, Scarlet danced left into the housing zone . . ."

It was early afternoon and most numans were either at work or in education centres. Macie was relieved that there was nobody on the streets to mock her non-orthodox style—numans never sang.

". . . Kohl splits the fork in the road seeking Lavender up the way . . ."

When Macie was a child, Vala had tried to explain the way numans navigated before they were old enough to be upgraded to full mapping functionality. Apparently, the city founders had incorporated architectural features into their buildings to help people find their routes. Vala had said that it was one of the few aspects of the city she found tolerable.

"See, the towers look like their names," she had said. "Quirky and cheerful."

Not to Macie. She realised long ago the decorations her grandmother loved must have been virtual. All buildings—Jade 3, Scarlet 8, Kohl 5, Lavender 1—looked depressingly grey to her.

". . . Citrone marks a step to the right, take a breath and beware. Amber's world can be busy. Chin up, don't despair."

Macie slowed down and steeled herself for the next street. Amber Road was a fearful place for Macie. Not so much because of the architecture, even though the colour palette was much bleaker than the rest of the city, but because it opened out onto the town square; the one place numans occasionally gathered en masse.

Despite their preference for virtual communications, the numans seemed to need physical proximity when Wolfram delivered important news. Or perhaps it was Wolfram himself that required the spectacle of massed underlings.

The mote, her little round techno-jailor, nudged her foot.

"Yes, I know. The wall's leaking, gotta be swift," she said, resuming her race.

Halfway down the road, a noise like a slow military drill rumbled towards her. Feeling a heavy dread, Macie's pace slowed as her pulse increased. Something was happening in the square.

A glance at her watch confounded her. It was too late for lunchtime exercises, too early for school let out. Emergency drills?

Three wary steps backwards and she was stopped by another barrage of sound. A troupe of at least fifty numans in worker overalls rounded the corner and marched down Amber, taking up half the width of the thoroughfare.

They shuffled towards her: footsteps synchronised with unnatural precision, eyes fixed on some unseen point ahead of them, arms swaying slightly to an un-hearable beat.

Macie's palms grew clammy and, for a moment, she thought she might throw up. She moved back against the nearest building, bent over and gripped her knees. Her bag tumbled to the ground, stomach heaving, although little came out.

"Come on Mace, get it together. Breathe in. Breathe out," she whispered as she wiped her face on her sleeve and stooped to retrieve her bag.

"Citrone marks a step to the right, Citrone marks a step to the right, Citrone—"

An echoing click broke her attempt at concentration. All around, doors opened with a coordination free-minded humans could never achieve. A second wave of numans flowed out of the buildings, already in step with the first group before their feet had touched the ground.

Macey tightened her grip on her bag. The marchers now took up the full width of the street. She was swept up in their parade and corralled into the octagonal town square where they joined thousands of numans gazing up at their Mayor being broadcast on a two-story display screen.

"Welcome, friends! Thank you for deviating from your workplans to attend this unscheduled gathering," Mayor Wolfram's voice boomed out of the screen. He wore the standard numan uniform like the rest of the population, yet his clothes seemed to be tailored to a higher standard. The fabric was clean and bright. His collar stood up crisply and appeared to glint in the sunlight.

All around her, numans were mouthing soundless platitudes and bowing slightly to their undisputed king. Wolfram responded by extending his strong arms like an ancient God bestowing shelter over his worshippers.

"I know many of you would have preferred to do this in virtual. Verbal comms are so primitive! Unbearably slow, right? Well, sometimes we have to go old-tech to value the new. How can we appreciate our glorious march up the evolutionary bridge, to an astonishing future now well within our grasp, if we don't look around occasionally to see the pathetic past we were lucky to escape?"

Goosebumps skipped down her arms. Macie knew this was only a one-way electronic broadcast, and most probably being piped directly into the minds of those who couldn't be physically present, yet she could not shake the feeling Wolfram was looking directly at her as he spoke those last words.

"Plus, I heard someone very special would be joining us here today. More about that later. Let's get on with our assembly!"

Wolfram clicked his fingers and pointed to the far side of the square. A ripple of heads swivelled around to see what he was indicating.

Macie looked too. She saw only the thickening cloud cover. The crowd must have been seeing a digital overlay as they all gasped in appreciation. A slow clap began in unison, ending with a ripple of nodding that cascaded through the crowd — high praise from the emotionally-closed numans.

As one, they turned their gaze skyward.

"That display was for you. And you, and you," Wolfram bellowed as he pointed to random members of the crowd. Macie followed their eyes but couldn't see anything.

"Thank you. You are all too kind . . . No, no, I'm only revealing the truth. You guys are the best!" he hollered in response to what Macie assumed were virtual comments pouring out of the crowd.

"A small token of my appreciation for all your recent efforts getting us back on track!" Wolfram smiled and waved. He pointed to the left, pretending his index finger was a gun. The crowd gasped. He pretended to blow smoke from his fingertip and mimed its return to a gun holster. The crowd laughed.

"I've got to get out of here," Macie muttered to herself, searching for an easy exit point. She elbowed her way back through the crowd, but there were so many of them, and with each of Wolfram's platitudes they surged forward, taking her with them until she was positioned only an arm's length away from the main screen.

At such close proximity, Wolfram's features were distorted. His middle-aged skull bulged to monstrously inhuman proportions. Veins erupted from his ports like thick snakes that pulsed up towards his temples. His black hair was pulled back into a regulation male plait, exposing his ears which looked large enough to hear every last footstep in the city.

"Now, to business—*and* our important guest. Three days ago, I alerted you to the missing one hundred grams at the Reclamation Centre. I'm sad to say, this isn't the first time." Wolfram frowned. The numans fell silent.

"We all know a small loss in isolation doesn't have much of an effect. One hundred grams equates to about half a cup of numan waste. In fact, you'd have to have two thousand grams to equate for one adult body being processed through the centre, but in a closed loop every resource *must* be applied strategically.

"What may be a few grams today, could be a few kilograms next year. Then what are we to do? Who amongst you will volunteer for the Reclamation Centre? Who will plug the resource leak?"

"A-ccount . . . re-cycle . . . re-claim!" The numans spoke with stilted syllables in eerily unison.

"That's right, only through dedication will we plug the leak and keep tracking upwards into a prosperous future for all numans!" Wolfram pounded his fist into his palm as he spoke.

"Now, I recognise that many of you have reached up for a solution to this problem, yet one of you stretched a little further. One of you chose to take a step higher on the ladder of righteousness to resolve the issue for the sake of the community.

"After three days of fruitless searching, one officer took responsibility for the lost grams. That officer was willing to stem the tide of our losses. They volunteered to make a reclamation on your behalf so that no other numan would have to go without."

The camera zoomed out to show Wolfram standing outside the entrance of the Reclamation Centre. Macie gasped. It was the very place she had stood three days earlier. Only Wolfram didn't have to whistle to gain entry.

"That's right, you're going to meet her now. Come forward and reveal your dedication to numanity!"

The door opened to reveal a familiar officer shuffling forward. Wolfram greeted her and lifted her arm to the sky in a victorious salute, but he wasn't smiling anymore. His eyes flashed dangerously and his forehead morphed into bitter stone. He appeared to glare directly at Macie.

One by one, all the numans in Macie's immediate vicinity turned to look down at her, their foreheads frowning just like Wolfram's and their fists clenched as though ready to pummel her.

Macie only vaguely perceived their threat. She recoiled in horror from the image on the screen, blindly batting at the arm of the nearest numan.

The crowd moved in closer and for a moment, it seemed as though night had arrived early. All around, the square seemed to be shrouded in deep black shadows.

Macie fell to her knees.

Wolfram's tone hardened. "No one is above the law—there is always a price to be paid for deviation. All leaks will be plugged, no matter the cost. Now return to work, all of you. Let this be the last we hear of missing grams."

The numans shuffled away with surprising speed. A few moments later, the square was empty, leaving the big display locked onto the last static image.

Macie wept.

The reclamation officer in the frozen image was Vala. It was her hand Wolfram had raised in the air, showing the bleeding stump where her last three fingers had been taken. Freshly reclaimed.

CHAPTER THREE: LOST

Macie didn't need to sing to find her way through the rest of the city to her workshop. Three motes herded her in the right direction with a series of small shocks. Truthfully, without them she would have continued to lay on the cold black pavers, weeping beneath the image of her grandmother's mutilated form.

As she trudged through the city, eyes clouded by disbelief and her mind a thousand miles from the leak, Macie barely noticed four large delivery motes speeding by.

When she passed her home address on Emerald Alley, she didn't care that they were loading boxes out of the goods lift, nor did she stop to examine their cargo. Just putting one foot in front of the other was a struggle.

By the time she arrived at her workshop, tears had rinsed her eyes clear of shock and remorse had taken over. It was a bitter companion; relentless in its stream of questions.

How had Wolfram known about their mission? Was she spotted on the roof? Were they watching her on the wall? Where did she make her mistake?

Zap.

Another sting to her right heel. She knew the motes were not going to let up until she completed her workplan. Resigned, Macie used her hip to shove aside some heavy boxes that were blocking her access to the workshop and used a key to unlock the old-fashioned wooden door.

It wasn't uncommon to have a few crates around the alleyway. The workshop was located in a tiny lane at the industrial end of the city and—unlike the rest of perfectly tidy DarwinTwo—raw materials were sometimes stacked haphazardly around her squat little building. It felt like a dumping ground for the lost or temporarily unnecessary.

Even the motes tended to ignore the lane. Of course, they continued to sweep behind Macie as she moved in and out of the area, but a quick scan down the alleyway at the dirt between the boxes revealed their priorities.

Stepping inside, Macie moved straight to her supply shelves. Normally, she loved her rare visits to the workshop. A leak was an excuse for a few minutes' respite from the numans' perfectly ordered world. She loved the way the wooden floors moaned a little under her steps. The whole building was charming in a cold, gritty way.

Its scale was more human than the rest of the city too. Six strides in any direction would have her colliding with a wall or workbench. A small vertical jump would allow her to touch the storage mezzanine.

It would have been an interesting piece of architectural history, had the numans been interested in history. Instead, it was an almost forgotten relic, tolerated as long as it served its purpose—a stop-off point for repair materials.

In truth, she could have used a much smaller space. Macie only needed a handful of supplies to do her repairs. She looked around at the clutter of redundant materials and regretted that she hadn't given a thought to sending them in for reclamation, but the motes left her little time for exploration. No time to examine the lengths of timber, cans, and jars of keys for non-existent locks.

A loud tap of an impatient mote at the door reminded her to get to work. As she mixed the repair

22

formula, the events in the square circled her mind.

Why didn't they tell me? I could have repaid a hundred Emilys with all this stuff, she thought in frustration, kicking at an old tin bucket that sat under the end of her workbench. It nudged a broom that fell against some leather-covered books and caused a cascade of shifting items.

Macie stooped to pick up a wrench and a length of rope that had uncoiled in the spill. Her hand lingered, feeling the coarse interwoven strands. She wondered if Vala still had the boat building book. Perhaps they could—

Bang!

A none-too-subtle knock of a mote butting her door reminded Macie that motes could not open low-tech doors. No resources were wasted on swipe pads or auto-openers for a lowly human.

They don't know what's here.

Bang! . . . Bang!

The dropped objects could wait, the motes wouldn't. She finished the formula, wiped her hands on her overalls and packed her bag, ready to complete the repair workplan.

***

Outside, a soft buzzing drew Macie's attention. Across

the lane, a ridiculously old comms station on an even older wooden pole—complete with a curved light hanging above it—was making a noise. The pole was an artefact from a time when two sets of initials joined by a heart apparently meant something, as someone had carved them over and over.

For Macie, it only meant trouble. The comms station on the pole was her only other communication point with numan society, beyond the motes and Vala. And it was ringing for the first time in four years.

She shoved three more boxes out of the way to get close enough to press the 'on' button on the comms station.

"Hello? Wall Manager Macie here."

The palm-sized comms screen crackled into life. A face peered at her expectantly. It was numan, no surprise there. Possibly male, always difficult to tell. Pale skin and severe regulation plaits made them all appear so similar.

"Yes, hello? Hello!" Macie repeated.

The numan opened and closed its mouth three times in fast succession as though in hurried silent prayer.

Macie sighed and pushed her loose hair off her face.

"Is there something wrong with this transmission? I'm not getting any sound at my end."

"Right, I was sub-vocalising. Habit. Forgot you don't do vir-tual," the numan uttered in the same stilted speech as Vala. "City Accommodation Manager Anderson here. Be advised your permanent housing has been reallocated to the Wall Management Workshop. This council directive will reduce your work commute and thereby increase workplan optimisation."

"What?"

"We have relocated all your possessions."

Macie looked at the boxes she had just moved with growing understanding. "Hang on, you can't do that. I live with my Grandmother!"

"You obtained your legal majority one year ago. You have no further need for contact with her."

"There's no room in there. It's a dirty workplace, not a home."

"It is sufficient for you."

"My grandmother needs me!"

"Numans only need the BigDry and you have no more need of familial supervision. Vala has been informed. Further discussion will delay your workplan. End communication."

"Wait—"

The screen turned off. No amount of pleading would bring it back to life.

***

Back at JK-97, Macie should have been worried that the

leak had worsened. More pieces of the ancient wall had flaked away, expanding the trickle into a small, but determined stream the width of two of her fingers.

She knew she should have been concerned that she might not have made enough repair formula or that it might not hold given the volume of wetness. Yet she wasn't.

Whatever, she thought.

Macie began her work by using a pointed trowel to push the formula into the break beneath the ring. She applied several layers, but each time a small leak would squirt out from the edge of the repair. Using a chocking bluestone fragment to buttress the wall would have helped, yet she couldn't work up an appetite for caring.

The two motes that had been trailing her backed away from the puddle that was growing around her feet. One dashed indoors, returning with a numan who stood like a sentinel inside the glass door of the closest building.

Let them watch.

Standing in the puddle had left her thin shoes vulnerable. Her numan cast-offs from Vala were not made for anything more than a sprinkle of water. Her feet were soaked along with the cuffs of her pants. Macie ignored it and continued slapping grouting formula onto the weeping wall; doing the bare minimum to complete her workplan.

Not able to stem the flow, she placed her hand over the repair and pushed against it to force the grout inside.

A tapping noise caught her attention. She glanced over her shoulder to see a second numan had arrived behind the glass. It knocked its finger on the pane of glass as it pointed at her, shaking its head.

And now you take an interest in me?

Locking eyes with the numan, Macie removed her hand with a theatrical flourish. The grouting came away, stuck to her palm, and water squirted out in even greater volumes. Despite their safe position, the numans flinched. The second mote spun around and whirled inside to join its companions.

Macie threw her head back and laughed.

Fools beware.

She held her wet hand skyward and squinted at the trickle that flowed down her sleeve. The water had a glittering sheen to it. The feeling of its trail along her skin was invigorating in a way nothing numan had ever been. She licked her fingers and its tangy salt revived her. A new idea flashed through her mind.

Let them taste it.

She started to do mental calculations about how long it would take for the leak to become a full breach. Whether it would reach her fourth-floor home, or what had been her home.

Home? Vala.

The bitter taste of old regrets replaced the fresh sting of seawater. She knew what she had to do.

With new enthusiasm, Macie rifled through her workbag and found a caulking peg in a pocket at the bottom. She used a soft mallet to pound it firmly into the grouting between the leaking stones. The stream immediately stopped.

Then she applied more formula over the top, and—for good measure—used a rounded trowel to smooth it over. She stepped back to review her handiwork, confident that the patch would dry and the JK-97 breach would be forgotten.

Soon, even the puddle at her feet was draining away, the signal the motes needed to leave their glassed safety and approach her position.

"Workplan complete. Leak repaired. Threat of further breach minimal. Wall Manager Macie out," she spoke to the closest one.

The report must have been relayed to the watching numans as they retreated from the windows. The motes returned to sweeping the ground, carefully avoiding the remaining wet patches.

Above her, the shards of sunlight were disappearing from the stormy sky. A dirty dusk was fast approaching and there was not a glimpse of blue to be seen. It dawned on her that she had never seen a numan looking skyward. She wondered if they knew what they were missing.

Still looking at the darkening clouds, Macie abandoned her tools on the ground, stepped over her work bag and climbed the nearest ladder.

On the top of the wall, she took one last look over her shoulder at DarwinTwo before turning her back on the city.

And then, without hesitation, she took a long stride forward and plunged into the sea.

CHAPTER FOUR:
THE COLOUR OF REDEMPTION

When Macie was small enough for the city to seem full of wondrous potential, when she hadn't heard words like *incompatible* or *reclamation*, and her biggest concern was whether she could jump down three steps at once without skinning her knee, her mother had taken her on a rare picnic with her grandfather, Wall Manager Roy.

It was a time before numans had officially become "numans" although, as a junior member of the city council, her mother already had a permanent digital port at the base of her skull.

While Roy and Macie picnicked, her mother spent the afternoon ensconced in the online world.

Occasionally, she would nod at her young daughter's babble. Mostly her eyes were glazed over, lost to unseen digital vistas.

Grandpa Roy, Macie's father's father, had no interest in technology and revelled in the natural world. They had spent the afternoon examining the old adjuncts and watching for mermaids who were known to sneak in on floating islands to abduct giggling girls.

He taught her that storm clouds rolled in from the north; a red dawn warned of a troubling day; and waves came in sets of seven—the last always being slightly larger.

It was a blissful afternoon. Best of all, he made her a salad of crisp green apples and juicy red berries—lavish treats in a diet that was increasingly grey.

***

Macie held her breath and sunk down into the cold embrace of the ocean, not caring what might lie beyond the wall. She didn't care that Wolfram would be inconvenienced, that somehow they would have to find a numan to devolve into a lowly Wall Manager.

Numans could have their world. The heavy black weight of woe was pushing her into the next world. She could only hope that it would be over quickly and that she would soon see Grandpa Roy.

When her feet first hit the water, she clenched eyes shut and crossed her arms over her chest for dramatic effect, imagining she would sink like a stone. After a few seconds, when she didn't feel the sea floor beneath her toes, Macie opened her eyes and was disappointed to see the surface was receding more slowly than she had expected. Her descent was slowing almost to a hover.

Frustrated, she waved her hands to push herself lower and was surprised at how thin the water felt. In all her years of gazing down into the ocean, she had not seen a hint of sea floor. She had assumed the water must be very thick at the bottom like grouting formula. How else could it look so opaque?

Macie moved her hands around her, delighting in the tickly caress of liquid as it rushed between her fingers. Much like the leak in the wall, it sparkled up and down her bare arms. She fancied that it was inviting her to play.

In her peripheral vision, a golden thread danced through the ocean. Macie swirled around, trying to get a better look, but it stayed just out of sight. She dived lower and a flash of rainbow raced past her left side. It was enough for her to continue the chase.

She spun a full circle, then tumbled head-over-foot before her forehead connected with a large boulder on the bottom. Rubbing her head, she realised her folly.

You're hallucinating, Mace.

No, Joy! Words bellowed through her mind from somewhere beyond her skull.

Well, it wasn't exactly those words. If she had to explain it later she would have been hard-pressed to verbalise the communication, but, just as knew the city was always abysmally beige and the ocean calming blue, right in that moment she knew a rainbow had flooded her mind with the clear expression of joy.

Shocked, she stopped. Her heart demanded she rise and breathe. Her lungs agreed emphatically, yet she overruled them both.

Joy. Came another communication, voiced with a brighter rainbow this time. She blinked to make sure she was seeing her surroundings clearly.

It was true. Everywhere around her, streams of colour were weaving through the currents. First, curious apple green; next, delightfully cheerful berry. Colours long forgotten and rarely tasted by Macie, bringing back memories of her glorious afternoon with Roy.

Time, the voice said warmly.

For a brief moment, she felt a push from below and wondered if Roy's mermaids would appear by her side. Instead, a swell of deep crimson rushed up from beneath, whispering so many emotions but yelling only one idea; *redemption.*

Macie surrendered and lay back in the water. She stretched her arms out, fingers and toes tingling with comprehension, and allowed herself to be pushed upwards.

Gasping, she breached the surface and gulped at life-giving air, flush with the realisation that it was not her ending after all.

CHAPTER FIVE: NEW OLD FRIENDS

It's funny how much your story can change with one small step.

Yesterday, everything seemed so hopeless. My life was empty. The motes treated me like a prisoner in my own city. Then being moved here—I couldn't imagine making a home alone amongst the hardware and dust. And what they did to Vala!

I kept thinking, this isn't the last of it, Mace old girl. Sooner or later they'll stop needing you and then what? Wolfram will have me furnaced into the raw materials for numan lunch, chairs or worse—maybe I'd end up a new comms port in the base of his ugly skull. How I'd make him itch if that was my fate. It would almost be worth it.

No, I wasn't going to quietly comply while they figured out a way to exit me, so I did it. I stepped off the wall. And you know what, it wasn't that bad. Really.

I've always found the water calming but being immersed in it was wondrous. I felt colours I haven't experienced since my childhood and something spoke to me through the water, showing me another possibility. A way out. It sounds crazy, I know. I wish I could ask Vala about it.

Anyway, when I got back here, drenched but alive, a second wondrous thing happened. I was scrounging the workshop for a towel when I found this Wall Manager's journal.

It was in a secret cavity behind some boxes. They must have started hiding it around Upgrade 14 when Wolfram made private book ownership illegal. I'm so glad they did. It goes back from Grandpa Roy to ten earlier generations.

The stories of those who have gone before me are giving me the hope I need. There's nothing like a little history to shine a light on your future.

I wonder, whose history am I?

Wall Manager Macie, Upgrade 24

Macie closed the journal, put her pen to rest on the table, and surveyed the workshop. Only three of the walls were wood. The fourth was the bare bluestone of the sea wall. When she edged her seat back and rested her head on the stone, she could hear the whispering tide on the other side.

It was strangely hypnotic. Within a few minutes,

she found herself swaying slightly with each swoosh of water. Perhaps she would enjoy her new digs.

A scan through the journal informed her that she wasn't the first Manager relegated to the shop. Lucas Johnson had been forced to take refuge in the small building during an uprising after Upgrade 6.

Already, she had taken Lucas' advice on heating; erecting a temporary screen around a camp bed to trap her own body heat and stave off drafts. She was looking forward to reading his other hints on making the rugged place a home.

A rumbling deep at her core reminded Macie that City Accommodation Manager Anderson paid scant regard to her nutritional needs. She'd stretched the previous day's rations as much as she could, but a meal was definitely the next item on her to-do list.

She opened her door to the deserted lane.

"Hey!" she yelled.

One person-shaped shadow moved slowly past an opaque window in the adjoining building. Nothing else. It was easy for Macie to imagine that she was completely alone in an empty city.

She closed her eyes and listened to the call of the ocean again. The idea of jumping back in made her giddy. Could she? Would she be detected? It had been hard to dry off after the last plunge even though it had been a warm evening. Today was cold. How would she explain wet clothes and hair to the motes?

Her belly interrupted her thoughts with another complaint.

"Quiet," she said to herself and stepped heavily over her threshold. One step. Nothing. Two steps. A mote dashed out from behind one of the boxes she was yet to unpack.

"What took you so long?" She bobbed down to look directly into its lens. "Message for Mayor Wolfram. If you want your wall maintained you'd better keep me in working order and that means food. Send some rations down here—fast. Wall Manager Macie, out."

The mote sped off and was swiftly replaced by another, quietly humming by her heel, ready to erase any errant DNA. Macie ignored it and strolled around the alleyway.

Looking in the boxes, hoping for some protein bars, she wondered how she was going to store all her possessions in the new smaller space. Admittedly it was only a few boxes worth, but the shed was tiny compared to the apartment.

She stopped foraging and leaned back against the comms pole. The workshop roof looked to be in pretty good shape, given its years of numan neglect. If the journal was any indication, it had to be at least three hundred years old. The original craftsmen had certainly known what they were doing. The walls were perfectly square. It had covered gutters, a sturdy chimney and it was roofed in thick grey shingles.

Macie wished the workshop had a proper second floor—not just a short storage mezzanine. She wondered how difficult it would be to extend it, after all it had a pretty steep roof; there had to be more room.

Then something occurred to Macie. She rushed inside, slamming the door behind her to stop the mote following. At the back of the room was a stack of building materials and spare stones covered in tarps.

In all her years of managing the wall, she had never given the pile a thought as her visits were short and moving the pile always looked like a major job. Macie smiled, realising that was exactly what had been intended.

She reviewed the internal space with new appreciation. It was smaller inside than out and there was no internal fireplace. So why the chimney?

Macie set to moving the tarped pile, but each way she pushed or pulled, nothing would give. No single piece of timber nor square of stone would budge no matter how much of her weight she threw at it. Someone had packed it in tight. It was as though it was all mortared together.

"Think Mace, think," she said, pacing the floor.

A crowbar rested conveniently against the wall. Macie picked it up. It was heavy in her hands and tarnished with age. Strangely, the chiselled end was clean as though it had been used often in its lifetime.

"Aha!"

There were scratch marks on the floor, approximately the size of the bar. Grinning, she stuck the bar in the location of the scratches and pushed with all her strength. She tried repeatedly to lever the stack from the wall, to no avail.

Defeated, Macie dropped the useless tool clanging to the ground and sat down heavily, puffing. There had to be a way to move the stack. She was certain it was hiding something.

The journal.

Macie spun around on her chair and gripped the nearest bench to pull herself over to the book, assuming the answer must be contained within its ancient pages, when she noticed a roughness under her fingers. Peering under the bench, she spotted a loop of coarse rope. It was perfectly sized for a human hand.

Not being able to think of any reason to have a loop of rope hidden under a bench, she pulled it. At first, it resisted, then with a little more grunt, the rope gave way. The sound of mechanical movement clicked from the back of the room and the pile of supplies slid effortlessly forward, creating a human-sized gap next to the wall.

"Yes!" Macie scrambled into the hidden passageway.

It took a moment for her eyes to see through the gloom. There were no windows and only one entry point. She reminded herself to bring a torch next time, but she was too excited to turn back.

Once her eyes adjusted, she was thrilled to see shelves bursting with books and trinkets, presumably rescued from the recycling drives. There were a few framed holopics, three wedding rings, a brass-topped walking stick and a strange stone cross standing on a wooden base.

As tempting as the shelves were, an item at the end of the small room stirred her belly. It was a ladder stretching up to a little door in the ceiling. Careful not to slip in the dark, Macie climbed the six steps to the top, and with a light shove, opened the door. Gleaming daylight pouring down onto the workshop rooftop.

Blinking, Macie grinned wildly when she realised the old fake chimney was perfectly positioned to shield rooftop excursions from prying eyes. Better still, there was a walkway leading a short distance up to the top of the wall. From here, she would be able to get onto the wall whenever she liked without anyone ever knowing.

Macie couldn't believe that she had never been to this part of the wall before. She had only ever examined the bottom section from within the workshop. Now she was kicking herself for her oversight.

Then something magical caught her eye. Two hand-sized brass loops were joined onto the wall. She clambered over for a closer inspection and was astonished to see an adjunct which had not been dismantled. No mysterious archaeological remnants were encrusted in the wall here. No, this was the real thing. It was a full ladder that ran over the wall—which was slightly convex on the ocean side—and hidden in its shadow was a small jetty where a green vessel was moored.

The temptation to examine the rare craft was strong, but she suspected that the motes might be waiting at her door with food. *They can't get in anyway.* She overruled her growling stomach and climbed down to the boat.

It was a modest vessel, perhaps big enough for six people. The mast was peeling and a wire frame that might have once been covered with a fabric canopy to form a cabin was rusting. Yet the hull looked sturdy. It seemed to shimmer lime as it bobbed around on the gentle current.

Macie sat on the edge of the dock and put a

tentative foot out towards the vessel. Beneath the cracking paint, the timber felt solid. She stretched her leg out and banged her heel firmly. With a loud crack, the edge of the boat deck gave way and Macie's foot sliced through the water.

Immediately, the sea rose up to splash at her exposed leg, and—just like last time—she felt alive with a rainbow of tingling sensations.

A larger wave washed up out of nowhere. It crashed over the dock and pushed her down onto the weathered boards, wetting her to the skin. A wash of cheeky turquoise made her giggle with glee.

A second swell rose out of the water, squeezing up between the planks and causing the water level to rise enough to lift her whole body a few centimetres above the deck. She trailed her hands through the water; fingertips brushing the wooden planks below.

The water invaded her ears and curled around her drifting hair, stretching across her forehead and rocking her into a dream-like state. It embraced her whole form as naturally as Vala's hugs.

Macie lifted one hand and watched as the water dripped away. She marvelled at how iridescent it looked in the early evening light. It was as though the water was shot through with deep burnt orange tendrils, just like the lipstick Vala had worn in the old holopic.

Yes, Kin! A deep voice reverberated through her mind, shocking her into sitting up. Immediately, the swell broke and drained back down into the sea. Assuming she had drifted asleep, she rubbed her eyes and coughed a little.

No. She imagined a gentle voice as the last drops of water receded from her face. Her stomach growled, loudly.

"Got to get some food Mace, you're starting to hallucinate again, old girl."

As she stood to leave the dock, she heard a roaring sound behind her. Macie turned to see a wave, almost as tall as a person, break from the rest of the choppy sea. It rushed towards her, rustling as it travelled, sounding more like a rumbling machine than water in motion.

Kiiiin! Kiiin! Kin, Kin, Kin, it whispered over and over, chugging as it closed in on her position. She knew this was no ordinary wave, it moved with menacing intent, yet she was mesmerised. Her feet seemed welded to the dock.

Kiiiin!

The wave struck the dock and its form disintegrated, leaving her in a shower of gentle droplets, each one shining with golden streaks.

We are Kin, it said in a voice that was both gentle

and determined. Then she knew. She smiled in wonder as she watched the sea settle back into a normal rhythm.

Stomach still rumbling, chest heaving with exhilaration, Macie turned and looked up to the tops of the city buildings rising just beyond the wall. For the first time in her life, they weren't beige. From the small jetty, the metropolis appeared to have a hopeful hue that shifted from gold to violet as she tilted her head from one side to the other.

Certainly a trick of the setting sun, she thought, totally delicious all the same. Vala would have loved it.

CHAPTER SIX: HOPEFUL DAYS

For many days, Macie's mind was awash with boats and whispering waters. If she could only find that old boat book, perhaps she could repair the vessel and acquire the skills of yachting to whisk Vala away from Wolfram's reach.

The problem, she reminded herself, was having somewhere to go. In her lifetime, there had been no indication of life outside DarwinTwo. No birds flying overhead. No visiting vessels. No noise from a distance. No smoke on the horizon.

But an entry in the journal said otherwise.

The last albatross left today. I watched it fly off to the north—its great wingspan beating into the thermals above our city, spiralling high into the sky, on its way to cruise the heavenly altitudes.

I'm not surprised it chose to leave us, following the last ship on the great journey to the other island.

My sister Pip was on-board. She always was too kind-hearted for what we must become. Pip was quite dramatic about her decision. She said she chose to embrace the uncertainty of the wild rather than the certain bleak entombment of machines.

Most of my colleagues believe the island to be a myth created by the Wolfram clan to lure the weak-minded to their demise, leaving greater resources for those of us who remain behind. I'm not convinced, but there is no choice for me. My Paul stays and therefore I must too.

Now I've been ordered to strip the wall bare of all landing points and fortifications. The official line is the need for recycling, which is absurd—we have abundant resources for the five hundred souls who remain.

I will do as I am bade, with one exception. I have decided to maintain the Wall Manager's Jetty with its twin vessels. Officially, it will allow for external examination of the wall. Unofficially, who can say.

And here I am on that very jetty, the last outcrop, watching her ship leave. I am ashamed to say I am howling like the old holopics of dingo packs, completely and utterly bereft.

Wall Manager Ewan, Upgrade 2.

It was late evening when Macie finally closed the old book and stowed it in the secret shelves of the back room. She wondered about Pip's fate on the endless ocean. Had it welcomed her as warmly as it had welcomed Macie? Did it reveal its colours to her?

It was a topic she needed to discuss with Vala. Some days, she felt like she was going mad. She would skirt around the city looking up at the towers and feel so little. Then one foot in the wash and she would be swamped by the heartache of childhood—the yellow ribbon she wore to her mother's funeral and the silver lightning that flashed through the sky the night Wolfram had renamed humanity.

Knock, knock.

Macie jumped. The noise was such a rare intrusion that at first, she didn't know what to make of it. *Possibly a package bumping against the wall? No, too loud.*

It couldn't be motes. Her workday was over and they would do the rounds by themselves until morning. Unless there was a leak to be repaired . . .

Knock, knock, knock.

Right, that was no accidental bump. There must be an urgent leak, she thought to herself. "Coming," she hollered, while she grabbed for her workbag and opened the door.

"Right, where is it?" she said, pulling on her work

boots and looking down at the mote. Except it wasn't a mote.

Instead, she saw numan shoes. And in the shoes was a numan who blinked too often and thrust out his hand like a small weapon of forced civility.

"Hello."

For a moment, no-one spoke, and the numan looked back and forth between his outstretched hand and Macie's hands that had landed firmly on her hips.

"This is still customary, is it not?" He spoke much more fluidly than her grandmother or the Administrator.

Macie knew the numan was a 'he' only because of his Adam's apple which was pushing through his waxy, tight skin; the kind you see on males who have a sudden growth spurt at the end of their adolescence.

"Well?" he said, holding his hand out to a stunned-silent Macie.

Shaking hands was a strange old custom she had never had an opportunity to practise. Numans rarely made physical contact. This offered hand was thin and pale, probably cold to the touch. She ignored it and plunged her own hands deep into her pockets.

"What do you want?"

"Right," he said, pulling his hand back. He didn't blush, but Macie felt certain she had embarrassed him. "I am Aaron, twelfth offspring of Mayor Wolfram. To complete my education and receive full upgrade into numan society, I must complete a work unit. I have requested and been approved for assignment to you."

"Why would you be allowed to study a lowly Wall Manager? Did you do something wrong? Punishment?"

"Not at all. I thought it might be helpful to study the wall. I shall review your management routines, debug your processes and identify workplan improvements. It will be a great opportunity for you to improve your primitive human skills. Of course, you could refuse."

Macie studied his body language as he spoke the last insult, wondering if he understood half of what he was proposing. Refuse? She knew she had absolutely no choice in the matter.

"When will this great opportunity begin?" she said drily.

"Tomorrow at twelve noon. I have classes to attend each morning, and the afternoons will be free for the wall project."

"Aren't you afraid? You'll be at risk of water contact, you know."

"Aren't you?"

Numan and human stood regarding each other for a few uncomfortable moments. Then Macie gave him a short fake smile, before turning and shutting the door behind her with an exaggerated firmness.

"Right, bye then," she heard Aaron's muffled voice, then his footsteps receded.

Macie held her breath and stomped her foot on the floor several times until she felt her calmness return. She had made up her mind. Somehow, she would find a way to see Vala.

CHAPTER SEVEN: DIFFICULT NIGHT

Back around Upgrade 21, when I was young enough to care about trivial things like human conversation, I spent three weeks trying to provoke my numan grandmother into chatting.

I'm ashamed to say, I started the campaign with a ridiculous display of holding my breath. The sting of Gran's hand on my cheek ended that in a few short minutes.

Next was a hunger strike which lasted fourteen hours and only garnered a grimace from her. Escalating levels of temper tantrums, tears, door slamming, and impotent threats of self-harm followed.

Returning home with an ancient boat building book drew a chuckle. Slamming the book against her bedroom door attracted nothing more than a deep sigh.

Only when I made a show of completing room re-allocation

forms on real old fashioned paper, did Vala finally break out of her trance. She tapped the tech port at the base of her skull, deactivating her links, then crossed the room with unusual haste.

Her eyes glistened as she wrapped me in a rare hug and spoke rapidly into my ear.

"Loved one, be careful. This cannot end well. We are watched all the time, you and I. Keep the light places lit in your heart but outwardly you must demonstrate numan acquiescence. I could not bear to see you in the Reclamation Centre."

A second later it was over. She pushed me out of her arms and reactivated her link to the BigDry. The spark faded from her eyes, and she shuffled away.

Wall Manager Macie, Upgrade 24

Three steps into her rooftop trek and Macie was already regretting her decision. It was late summer, the sky was clear, and as the evening cooled, dew had collected on the workshop's tiled roof, making every slippery step potentially lethal.

"Don't be a wimp, Mace," she whispered, daring herself to continue and wishing the moon was out.

When she reached the wall, she stopped for a moment and laid down to hug the ancient structure. The call of the ebbing tide vibrated up through the stones to her bare cheek. It whispered colourful ideas. She was tempted to scrap the mission and go down to the jetty instead.

"Keep going, Mace," she said, pushing herself up onto her hands and knees and resuming her crawl.

It was eight o'clock. Most of the numans would be home and deep into virtual entertainment or study. Still, there were lots of windows in the accommodation towers. She had to keep her profile low and her pace steady.

***

The City Distribution Hub was only about twenty minutes' crawl along the wall, yet the muscles in her lower back pleaded for a return to the workshop. Macie lay flat against the wall and took a moment to recover.

The sound of the hub was jarringly different to the ocean. To her left, she could hear the rhythmic swell washing her worries away. On her right, the clang and tick of mechanical devices in the hub seemed to warn; *Stand clear; no place for you.*

The small grey motes that monitored her movements all day were performing a similar role in the hub—constantly zipping between the larger units and comms stations, nudging the process along. At the far end of the warehouse, larger white delivery motes presented with empty trolleys and left stacked high with boxes.

At the entrance closest to her was a bay for the mammoth carriage motes. These were her quarry. The oversized vehicles had the capacity of a small room to transfer bulk materials to and from the Reclamation Centre, right by Vala's apartment block.

Macie heard one of the powerful beasts revving just inside the warehouse, likely limbering up for a delivery. She scrambled to its position and leapt the short distance to the warehouse eaves that stood about the same height as the wall. Three breaths later, the mote slowly emerged. She sucked up her courage and took one more leap—this time onto its back.

As it lumbered out of the hub, Macie found an air vent to grip. She held on tight and piggy-backed her way through the city, hoping she was heading in the right direction.

***

Two hours and two mote transfers later, Macie finally arrived at the Emerald Apartment Complex. The lateness of the hour had made it blissfully quiet. She slipped inside, unseen, then sprinted through the hallways to Vala's apartment. Just as she had hoped, Vala hadn't removed Macie's access to the palm scanner and she was able to enter with ease.

Inside, nothing much had changed. The furnishings remained in the same places—a photo of the city on one wall; shelves of crockery at arm's reach above a dining table on the other side; a two-person lounge facing the window . . . and one grey-haired lady sitting on an austere armchair.

"Gran!" said Macie, running across the room and embracing Vala from behind, hugging her shoulders and burying her face in her grandmother's greying hair. Macie knew she should have waited to make sure Vala wasn't in deep virtual, where a physical touch could come as quite a shock.

"I've missed you!" said Macie. "I'm sorry about your reclamation—I wish I'd been here to help you. Are you healing okay? Let me see your hand."

Without waiting for a response, Macie moved around in front of Vala and picked up her bandaged hand. She bent down and lightly kissed the dressings tinged with blue.

"It's all my fault."

She continued to hold Vala's injured hand in her own while she looked into her weary face. Her grandmother hadn't spoken yet, and her eyes were large with shock. Her usually white skin seemed to blush with surprise.

"Oh, I must have woken you out of the Dry. Sorry, Gran. It's just that I don't have much time—I don't think they'd want me in the city right now and I don't want to get you in any more trouble. Anyway, I had to find out about your hand as soon as I could find a way to get here. Does it hurt terribly?"

"You don't need to—"

"I know, Gran," said Macie, cutting her off. The words tumbled out of her like a raging waterfall. "But I do feel sorry about it. I feel awful, in fact. If only I could have explained or taken the reclamation in your place."

One of Vala's eyelids fluttered and her good hand gripped the arm of the chair tightly. An almost imperceptible whistle passed through the gap in her front teeth. Assuming it was stressful for her to talk about the incident, Macie swiftly changed the subject.

"Look, I need to ask you, did any of the family ever have vision problems? Hallucinations? Vivid dreams? For a while now, I've been seeing some pretty weird things. Amazing things actually. The water, it's— oh I don't know how to explain. Remember Grandpa Roy's stories of big colourful—"

"No! I am not a *lib-rary* Macie. Can't rush in asking about silly . . . human day-dreams. I've told you that before."

Macie recoiled from the uncharacteristically harsh remark. "It's important, Gran. I can't just plug in like a numan and get instant access to everything. I'm stuck in that workshop with nothing—"

"Mace!" Vala snapped.

"—and no-one to share my news."

"Stop and listen child! We have company." Vala was speaking more fluidly now. Clearly out of virtual, her eyebrows were raised as she looked to the other side of the apartment.

Macie turned slowly, her careless haste making her stomach churn.

He was standing in the doorframe, wiping his hands on a faded old handtowel. It was the numan who had approached her about working on the wall—Aaron.

"Hello again," he said cheerfully. He placed the towel on the bench and moved further into the room. "Your grandmother was kind enough to offer me use of her bathroom facilities. I'm rather glad I did, otherwise I would have missed your visit. News you said? That would be news of my wall project, right?"

Macie could only nod.

"That is exactly why I came to see your grandmother. As the matriarch of a family of Wall Managers, it made sense to start my research at the top. She was kind enough to fill me in on Roy, and David before him. You know, the sort of stuff you can't find in official records."

Macie watched Aaron's eyes flicker to the ceiling briefly—a sure sign he was accessing data.

"Funny, the motes should have let me know you were coming. Never mind—Vala has heard the news twice now. Thrice if you include the memo father sent."

Both Vala and Macie nodded.

"Right, well, goodnight Vala, we should let you get some rest now. It wouldn't do to have you falling asleep on the job tomorrow. Might end up misplacing a reclamation again."

Vala's eyes opened wider. Macie was still silent.

"Macie, father has sent a mote to see you home. This pesky city must be difficult to navigate with your—your *challenges* and all."

Aaron headed to the door and held it open, waiting for her to make a move.

"Um, yes, I'd better be off. Sleep well, Gran," Macie muttered as she hugged Vala and followed Aaron's path into the corridor.

At the door, blocking Aaron's view, Macie stopped to take one last look into the apartment where she had spent most of her life. She had a sickening feeling that it might be the last time she would see it.

Vala—who still had her back to the door—must

have sensed her hesitation. She swivelled her head towards Macie and, without taking her eyes off the door, made the briefest motion with her heel kicking at something under her seat. The spine of an old book spat out from the underside of the couch.

For the briefest instance, their eyes met. Then Vala pointed to the book and winked, before pushing it back under the furniture.

Macie smiled; she had her answer.

CHAPTER EIGHT: SMALL TALK

Aaron has been shadowing me every afternoon for two weeks now. He gawks over my shoulder as I work and asks way too many questions, pretending to take paper notes on my every action—as if a numan has to write anything down.

Vala told me once that their ocular connection uploads continuously so everything they view goes into the central processor. Aaron claims his virtual connections won't be complete until he graduates. Until then, he only has limited search and comms capability. I'm not sure I believe him. Every so often I catch him gazing off into the distance, a sure sign of a BigDry connection.

He's scared of the water, by the way. I don't think it likes him either, but it's not scared like he is. Like all numans are.

At the end of the day yesterday, when he turned his back to climb down the wall, and I was feeling so relieved to see him go, a great swell of bright emerald water reared up and slammed into the wall. It was as if it was waving him away, or maybe giving him one last push back into the city where he belongs.

The overspray reached the back of Aaron's neck. He took out a handkerchief and frantically dabbed the port under his ear; lest the cruel water damage his precious circuits. He clambered down that ladder so fast he missed the last step and tumbled onto a mote.

Hilarious.

We stood there for a few minutes, me and the twinkling puddle of residual water. I've never seen a numan scramble like that; tripping over his feet as he escaped the scary water. Racing into the nearest building.

It was hard not to snigger. I so want to hate him.

Wall Manager Macie, Upgrade 24

A drop of water splattered on her page. Macie closed the journal and peered up at the ceiling. The rain had not let up since a storm rolled in just after dawn. When it stopped, she would have to figure a way to get up to the roof and patch the leak.

Until then, she was counting on having the day to herself. No numan would willingly risk water contamination. And the motes, they would keep their distance too—scurrying from window to window, reduced to passive observers.

She grabbed a protein bar, pulled her coat hood down over her head, then stepped outside. A mote was watching from behind a glass door in the building opposite. She slammed her foot on the ground, connecting with a deep puddle that splashed up her trouser leg.

"Wimps!" She laughed.

***

The trick to managing an ocean wall in a rainstorm was to look for unnatural patterns and volumes in water paths between stones. Macie spent the morning trying to spot such places and was lost in her work when the skies finally cleared and Aaron emerged from a nearby building, complete with boots, coat, scarf and umbrella.

"Hello, there," he said, looking not at Macie but up at the sky, hand outstretched checking for any errant drops.

"That should be the last of it," he said, snapping his umbrella closed with forced confidence.

"Really?" said Macie, turning back to her work. She had identified a weak spot in some grouting around DS-04 and was on her knees, working on a preventative patch.

"I've had an idea for next time though."

"Mmm," murmured Macie, not wanting to break her concentration on the wall.

"Yes."

Macie didn't respond.

"Look, is that important?" said Aaron.

"All wall repairs are important."

"Right, it's just that I have something to show you."

A shrug was all Macie gave to indicate her level of interest in his show-and-tell. A hopeful crack of yellow lightning signalled another cloud system approaching from the north. A large wave hit the wall and a fine spray made it over.

Aaron took an involuntary step backwards and began opening his umbrella.

Macie leaned forward and pressed her cheek up against the glistening wall. Her training taught her that it wasn't possible, yet she had a sense that she could feel the stones tremble against the churning sea.

She wondered what it would be like to leap off the wall again, to lose herself in the blissful rainbow of turmoil, to surf in the shimmery hue of freedom.

A clicking noise pulled her attention back to the city. Aaron was fumbling with his half-opened umbrella. The wind had picked up, causing the canopy to twist inside out.

"Looks like your forecasters were wrong; might want to scurry inside," she said in a dry tone, waving her trowel at him as she spoke.

"Lightning does not always equal rain."

A moment more of fumbling and Aaron finally got the item closed up and popped it under his arm. He sniffed, pushed his shoulders back, and swept his black hair into his regulation numan plait.

She wondered if the moisture in the air had short-circuited his doohickies; confidence matrixes, or whatever they called them. It made her smile to see a little colour sweep over his cheeks. With a bit more of a human tinge, he almost looked handsome.

"You sure you don't want to have this conversation tomorrow? Wouldn't want you to fry a circuit or anything." Macie got up off her haunches and tapped her foot in a nearby puddle, sending a splash onto Aaron's trouser leg. He flinched, then rolled his eyes in response.

"Of course not. I'm fine. We numans are not actually affected by water any more than you are, you know. We just *prefer* to be dry."

"Really?"

"Sure, back in the early days getting water in your neural implant was a definite worry. Then we had the faulty implants of Upgrade '04 that led to significant losses. Didn't anyone tell you about that?"

Macie shrugged indifferently and squatted back down to her work.

"There was a sudden downpour at the family day rally. Sixty-four people were fatally electrocuted, another two hundred suffered serious shocks. Took a while to recover from that.

"Upgrade '05 included hardware improvements that make it nearly impossible to be affected by water now—still, fear of water is deep in our psyche. Especially the adults who are linked into the BigDry. I only understand it academically from my history lessons of course, but I'm told they can experience a communal memory flashback to that day whenever it rains." Aaron shivered. "Living in a world decimated by floods doesn't help. It's an understandable communal phobia that should be respected and examined, not mocked."

Macie looked away.

"Anyway, father has resolved that all tech must be waterproofed from now on. We will no longer be held to ransom by the weather."

"Right."

"So, if I may, I have come to show you this."

Aaron walked over to the nearest building and opened the door. Out sped two normal grey motes and a new black mote. It was a similar shape and size to the standard motes, except for the addition of four articulated arms at one end and two at the other.

"Our engineers have been working on these for a while. When I saw it, I knew it would be perfect for the wall. Six arms. Impressive!" he said, beaming.

"How is that impressive?"

"Wait."

The black mote stopped in front of her and appeared to study her work. It made a little whirring noise, then snatched the trowel out of her hand with such force that Macie overbalanced and fell backwards onto her behind. She wasn't sure, as she wouldn't give Aaron the satisfaction of turning to face him, but she thought she heard him snigger.

The grey motes moved in closer to the wall as if to get a better view of their new colleague which was touching the wall tentatively with its two front legs. Then, as quickly as the last clap of lightning, it jumped onto the wet wall and began climbing up to the repair point.

"You're kidding me," she said, standing up and rubbing her eyes.

Aaron nodding smugly as he rocked back and forth on his heels.

The mote arrived at the repair site and began pushing grout into the wall just as another large wave hit, showering them all in salty spray. Aaron held his ground this time, but the grey motes tore off to the safety of the nearby building and the black mote lost its grip.

It fell to the ground with a loud crack. Its legs kicked in the air three times and a spark erupted from its belly before it became still and silent.

The sky chose that moment to unleash another band of drizzle. Aaron reached down and scooped up the mote, turning it over as if looking for the fault. Finding nothing obvious, he shrugged.

"Clearly the prototype still needs some work. Still, this was a useful test on a well-needed initiative."

"Needed by who?"

"You, of course. Us. The whole city. Repairs in the rain means foolproof protection against the ocean. Perfect!"

Macie picked up the dropped tool and used it to scrape up the remaining grout.

"Macie?"

She ignored him and kept working.

"What's wrong?"

When Macie refused to respond, Aaron shuffled from one foot to the other as if uncertain of his next move.

Macie then switched to a finer trowel which she used to smooth out the surface of her work with a deft flick of her wrist. She stood back to watch the colour lighten as the repair set.

They both stood silent for a moment, rain cascading down their faces, the only sound the raging sea beyond.

"Right, well, if your human deficiencies can't allow you to see the benefit of this initiative, I'm not sure there is anything left to discuss. I will see you tomorrow to continue our project."

"Your project," she corrected him.

"I would have thought 'ours' was the more appropriate pronoun considering all of DarwinTwo will benefit."

"All of DarwinTwo?" she said through gritted teeth.

"Of course! I'd say automated wall repair, even in rainy conditions, is a significant improvement. It's a major advance for the safety of everyone."

Macie reached down and made a loud show of returning her tools to her backpack, before turning her back on Aaron and storming off.

"Macie, talk to me. I thought we were doing this project together? I thought we were becoming . . . friends?" Aaron yelled after her.

Macie turned. He had reopened his umbrella and looked pathetic standing all alone under the darkening sky.

"What do you want me to say, Aaron?" she yelled back, taking a few small steps to close the distance between them. "Hope you get an A on your project, friend? Or thank you for reminding me, I'm just a tool. Easily replaced."

Aaron's pallor returned. "Ah, I never meant to—I never thought—"

"No, you numans never do, do you? And yet, there it is."

"But this efficiency advancement will support numans for centuries to come."

Macie moved closer. "Right. Like Upgrade 21. That was the year you guys started growing all embryos ex-utero. Such a great advancement for numankind. No more need for pesky motherhood. I'm guessing you were born after that upgrade? How are you enjoying that efficiency? You going to cuddle up to a computer bank and have a good cry about the failure of your black mote today?"

A gust of wind caught his umbrella and tore it out of his hand. They both watched it fly around the corner of the building, yet Aaron stood his ground.

"And where exactly is *your* mother, Macie?"

She was face-to-face with him now, close enough to feel his breath steaming in the cold. Her fists were balled and her muscles ached to strike.

"At least I was born to a mother who knew me and I grew up with a grandmother who taught me the value of all life. You numans took her away from me, too."

Aaron winced and looked down at the rivers of rain flowing around Macie's feet.

"That's what I thought. Excuse me, I have to get back to my workshop."

CHAPTER NINE: THE LAST MERMAID

Great Aunt Hae died today.

Her sister—my grandmother—says she died of salt sickness; a great longing for the caress of the tide which is forbidden inside this stone prison.

Of course, her problem was nothing so mystical.

The doctors say her body rejected the latest upgrade at a cellular level. The polarity of her ageing brain cells flickered back and forth struggling to incorporate the new electrical coding until they seized altogether.

She was not the only one incompatible with the upgrade. Eleven people had significant seizures, three fatal. There are renewed calls for the council to review the intracortical program.

I will miss Great Aunt Hae. She often joined me on my perimeter checks, telling me stories of the time before The Rise; when the world was drier, water was for play, and life had choices.

Sometimes, she would coyly place one foot on the lowest rung of a wall ladder and suggest we climb up to take in the view. "Can you hear? The whales are calling us," she would say, "let's take a quick look!"

I knew better. Grandmother had forbidden it. She said one splash of the devil's water would transform her sister into something more aquatic than human and with a flick of her tail she would disappear, lost to the castles beneath the waves.

After her funeral, I searched the genealogical archives in the City Library. I discovered that our Korean ancestors were the Haenyeo of Jeju—a tribe of women who had earned their living for thousands of years, diving deep into the oceans in search of food and aquatic gems.

I begin this journal in honour of Great Aunt Hae, surely the last of the mermaids. My hope is that all Wall Managers will record entries here. This book will be a dance back to our past while everyone else falls into the future.

Wall Manager Hyo-Sonn, Upgrade 1

Macie closed the old journal, laid her head down on one arm and explored the coarse grain of the old table with the other. Before she had moved into the workshop, she had never viewed the table as much more than a workbench aged by the toils of countless Wall Managers.

Now that the room had become her home, the bench had transformed into a combination writing desk, dinner table and dream space.

She drummed her fingers and a bright memory of Roy skipped into her mind. It was a cool day and he had been keeping her warm by teaching her to dance to a ditty about an octopus who was getting married to a mermaid, only he kept fumbling with the wedding ring, despite his many arms.

Remembering the golden afternoon with her grandfather made her smile, and soon she found herself tapping out the tune with her pen. Surprising herself at the rare display of musical ability, she reached up to the shelves and pulled down some empty resin tins to use as drums.

Next, a small jar of nails took her eye. She grabbed it with her other hand to add the syncopated tinkle of iron on glass, then tapped her foot against a joyously caramel water barrel under her desk. Overlaying a scat vocal sent her into a full jazz riff that left her gyrating in delight.

"What's that?" came a steely voice from behind her.

Macie dropped her improvised instruments. As she turned around, her heart took over the beat. Aaron was standing in the doorway.

"Oh. I. Um," she stammered, avoiding eye contact and frantically re-shelving her repurposed items.

"That sound. What do you call it?"

"What do you mean?"

"The noise."

"I don't hear anything. I'm cleaning. You're late."

Macie made an exaggerated show of shuffling more items than had been included in the music kit. Then she remembered her journal which was still in plain sight. She moved a hessian storage bag over it and pretended to use it to pack some small tools away.

"The sound before. I was knocking and there was no answer, so I opened the door. You mustn't have heard me over the racket you were making. When I came in you were—well I don't know how to describe what you were doing. It was like this."

Aaron waved his arms about and wiggled his hips in an approximation of Macie's orchestral moves. When she didn't respond, he cleared his throat and warbled a few notes.

"Surely I didn't look or sound that bad," she said fighting the urge to laugh.

"Maybe not."

The edges of Aaron's mouth curled slightly. Macie thought he might actually crack a smile. Instead, he straightened his lips into a numan grimace and stared briefly off into the distance.

"No, I've got nothing," he said. "Can't remember ever seeing anything like it. Please tell me."

Macie wondered if he had queried the central database. The possibility that Wolfram was viewing her through his son—observing her workshop for the first time with all its reclaimable materials—made her sweat. What would be the penalty for her stash? Where would she be sent to live next?

"I guess you numans deleted your manners algorithms. Let me assure you it is not good manners to enter a lady's home uninvited. Out. You wanted to observe me making a non-critical repair, let's go."

She grabbed her workbag off the back of her chair and tried to shoo him out the door. Aaron wasn't budging.

"Wait. I need to know. What was all that about? Please?"

She took her jacket off a hook on the wall and stretched her arms into it, hoping to obscure much of his view inside the workshop. Aaron folded his arms and rocked back on his heels. Macie pushed past him, forcing him to follow her and turn away from her room.

He stared at her silently.

She waited.

He raised an eyebrow.

Macie sighed. "Alright then, it's called music."

Again, Aaron's eyes changed focus briefly before returning to Macie. "Go on."

"I can't believe you've never heard of it."

"Until I become full numan, I'm required to spend all my spare time on studies. And that, whatever you did, is definitely not on the syllabus."

"I guess you could describe it as an old human recreation activity. No big deal, just a bit of fun. I'm sure you can look it up if you want to know more. Now, let's go. That adjunct is going to start leaking unless we do the maintenance."

"And exactly how am I going to 'look it up'? I can't ask any of the adults I know; if it isn't in our edu-modules then it's most likely forbidden. Asking about it could land me in a re-boot facility regardless of my lineage, and you'll end up in the Reclamation Centre for exposing me to non-essential concepts—not to mention all those hoarded resources in there."

Macie stepped back into the room, reaching behind him to the doorknob and raising her eyebrows, indicating her desire for him to move so she could close the door.

"Hoarding? That's a bit of a stretch. I inherited these items when your father made me Wall Manager. Now I have to share my space with them, living in a cold, grotty workshop because your kind kicked me out of my family home. If numans gave a damn about me, they would come and see how I'm getting along, wouldn't they? Do you have enough food, Macie? Are you cold or lonely, Macie? Have you even got a bed, Macie?"

Aaron swallowed hard.

"Am I wrong?" Macie almost snorted as she forced out her words. Then something astonishing happened. Aaron reached out and put his hand on her shoulder.

"I'm sorry. Do you want me to say something to father? Try to get your accommodation re-assigned?"

She shrugged away from his hand.

"Don't bother. I'm getting used to it, fixing things up the way I like them. Being closer to the wall is kind of helpful too, I guess."

"Actually, I needed to speak with you about that. I can't join you today. There's a big announcement going down. Probably new recycling targets or something equally dull. Anyway, all non-adults need to be in edu-centres to hear it."

"Really? They can't pipe it into your port, or whatever you call it?"

Aaron shook his head slowly and blinked as if she'd slapped him. "I've told you multiple times that I only have limited virtual access. Is your memory corrupted or are you this obstinate with everyone?"

"No, my memory is fine, thank you. It's just that you do this thing with your eyes which looks just like the adult numans when they are accessing virtual."

"I can't access the main systems, but I can do memory dumps. Organic memories are so corruptible, subject to constant revision by imagination and emotional layering. When I want to retain something important, I dump a copy in my internal memory core."

"You've been doing it a lot lately."

"This project is generating lots of memories I want to keep. Memories of you. I'm interested in the way you live and the way you are so free with your emotions. You're so different to numans. I like it. I don't want to forget you when I get access to the BigDry."

He gave her shoulder a quick squeeze. Macie flinched at his touch and took a step backwards, forcing him to break contact, but she couldn't help smiling, just a little. Aaron smiled back.

"Pity I don't have a hard memory space. A smiling numan; that's a keeper."

Perhaps it was the summer light reflecting off nearby windows, but for the briefest of moments, there was a blue glint in Aaron's black eyes. She wondered what he would look like relaxing on her little boat.

She had been working on the vessel most nights,

struggling to reproduce the repair techniques she remembered from the old boat book at Vala's. Now that the repairs were almost complete, sailing away to a place with real humans and fresh food was becoming her favourite daydream.

A mote dashed out of the alleyway and began scrubbing the small path she had travelled from her door. Aaron's body stiffened as though he had tasted something sour. He took a step away from her and cleared his throat.

"As I was saying, be advised that I will need to put the project on hold today. We will resume tomorrow. Have an efficient afternoon."

Without waiting for her response, Aaron spun on his heel and marched away.

CHAPTER TEN: FLUID MOMENTS

Madness is a desperate friend to those of us who toil alone.
He meets me at the weeping bricks and encourages me to moan.
He calls to me from the roaring depths with promises of kin.
Mirages of turquoise release my hopes and I am completely taken in.

Do not be swayed!
Though Kin may come smiling, he is no-one's friend.
Be not swept up by his folly, or madness will be your end.

Wall Manager Esmeralda, Upgrade 15

The afternoon crawled without Aaron's pestering. When Macie made her repairs, she found herself explaining her actions aloud as though he was there, observing and writing notes in his little black book.

The city was quiet too. There were no shadows moving behind windows, no workers changing shift. A solitary mote trailed her and by the end of her morning shift that one had disappeared too, leaving only the whistling breeze for a companion.

The silence of her workplace had never been so loud. It was easy to imagine the numans had all gone. Vanished. Uploaded into the heavens, leaving DarwinTwo to its one human beneficiary.

Suddenly cold, despite the heat bouncing off the white building behind her, Macie rubbed goosebumps out of her arms. She wondered if she had time for a few minutes of tranquillity on the top of the wall. The wide bluestones would be warm after soaking up the sun all day, the perfect remedy for chilly bones.

When she climbed the last rung on the ladder and poked her head over the wall, she was surprised to see the ocean so agitated for such a clear sky. Frothy tops of waves danced without rhythm, despite the still air. She put her hands on the hot stones and stretched up on tiptoes to see if there was a storm brewing beyond the horizon.

When Macie squinted and cocked her head to the left, she was able to fool herself that a flotilla of departing ships had caused the choppy wake. Perhaps it was Aaron at the helm, or maybe Grandpa Roy? She shook the ludicrous fantasy from her mind. If it was Roy, he would certainly be returning from distant shores, not leaving.

Warmer now, Macie finished her daydream and climbed the rest of the way onto the wall. She took her shoes off and hung her legs over the edge, hoping for the touch of sea spray.

Gazing down at the water far below her feet, she noticed the colour was ebbing with each incoming ripple. It was as though a cloud of ink was rising from the ocean floor, spreading into a person-sized stain. Initially, she mistook it for her own shadow until she realised the sun was slightly ahead of her, making her shade fall on the city side of the wall.

"What's this?"

A dark gelatinous wave top slapped against the wall and stretched up, unnaturally, to envelop her feet. It was like a cool satin sheet against her skin. It slid back and forth with the tide, making a sucking sound that was strangely musical.

Hush, it seemed to gurgle at her.

"Heatstroke?" Macie wondered.

Hush. Qui-et, the water warbled back.

Stunned, Macie retracted her feet and looked around for the source of the voice. She leant over the city side of the wall.

"You back, Aaron? Did you say something?"

No one in sight. Assured she was alone, Macie turned back to the sea, still unwilling to acknowledge what her instinct had suspected for some time.

Kin, it crackled.

"I'm hearing voices again. Gotta get out of this sun, Mace." She rubbed the sweat off her temples and turned to leave.

But the water shifted to emerald green and seemed to deliberately reach higher, stretching up to her ankles with a gentle stroke.

Kin here! it slopped.

"You. The water—you are Kin?"

Yessss, it hissed.

"No, I'm losing it," she said to herself, "they should have reclaimed me with the rest of my kind."

Kin, it said, louder this time, its consonants punctuated by a splash against the stones, showering her knees in droplets. They glistened with unnatural intensity, then slid back to join the whole.

Kin, Kin, KIN! The surface of the water rippled with a flush of dark despair. A muddy stain blossomed and grey bubbles erupted from below.

Not sure it was the right move, but unable to think of an alternative, Macie slowly extended her leg out and dipped one toe back in the turbulent water.

Yes, Kin gurgled.

As fast as a thunderclap, a bolt of intense colour flashed into her mind. Every cell in her body was flooded by a translation matrix of colour. The black of despair, a sunburst of orange optimism, breathless violets, powerful gold and a whole spectrum of peaceful life-affirming blues. It was a language of a clarity she had never experienced before. It felt like coming home.

Thank you for trusting, Kin. Human language is rigid. Difficult to construct sounds without anatomy. Physical contact allows colour communication through a neural link from our cloud-mind to your cellular mind, Kin conveyed in a rush of rainbow.

"What, how?" Macie's mind reeled at Kin's message.

The water soaking her foot shook out its response. *Cannot hold this form for long. Draining. We must hurry.*

"How is this possible?" asked Macie, overlaying vague, curious aqua thoughts over her words as she grew more comfortable with her new connection.

Hard to convey. Must seek knowledge.

"Where?"

Roy was a teller.

"You knew Grandpa Roy?"

Yes but weak connection. Macie / Kin better. Best! Macie moves quickly from colour expressions of emotion to abstraction. As long as we have physical contact, we can talk fluidly. Bliss!

Macie was quiet. She rubbed her hands through her hair as she searched for a logical explanation. She looked to the sky for an answer, but not even the strong sun could explain the exchange. "Why now?"

The abomination is quiet.

"Abomination?"

Kin's great foe beyond the stone. Too quiet. Worrisome.

The water on her foot began to shimmer like a muscle tremoring under strain from weights.

Can't hold.

"Wait, don't go," she begged.

The teller's stories hold the answers.

As quickly as it had begun, the connection was broken. The wave lost its form, splashing back into the sea, and—once again—she was alone.

CHAPTER ELEVEN:
PERILS OF KNOWLEDGE

Once, when I was about seven, Grandpa Roy had a great row with mother about the library.

I remember him yelling that every child deserved access to its volumes, especially if they weren't enrolled in school nor had any access to virtual eduguides. Mother said it was a waste of resources that would have been recycled years ago if it wasn't for nutbag constitutionalists like him.

I asked what an eduguide was. Grandpa rolled his eyes and said "nothing important" before scooting me outside to the corridor to play. Even with my ear pressed up against the door, I couldn't hear mother's response. She was in a very black mood when she left.

The next day, Roy took me to the library. People stared when we walked up the nine great steps to the entry foyer. City officials took Roy aside for a long discussion. They pointed at me, he pointed to the books and the fearsome stone eagle that crouched in the rafters.

While I waited for them to finish, a boy who looked to be the same age entered with no fuss at all; books firmly tucked under one arm, tongue poking out at me.

When we finally walked past the eagle I noticed it had a ribbon in its beak emblazoned with the words Cognitionis Computatrum Efficientium. I did not think to ask for a translation. I could only hold my breath and hope for all the world that it wouldn't swoop down and scratch my eyes out.

Wall Manager Macie, Upgrade 24

Macie had always thought Mauve 3 Street was a strange name for an avenue that housed the city's educational facilities. Sure, it was charming for the infant nursery at the top of the street and acceptable for the primary school, but the senior school and the city library vaults deserved a little more gravitas.

It was a pity numans didn't value history. She fancied the name of a city founder or influential leader might be more appropriate. Even Wolfram Way would be more impressive than Mauve 3 Street.

The sound of a door opening pulled her out of her musings. While the adult numans were lost to the upgrade, the unlinked minors were clearly not. Two youths were entering what she assumed would be the senior study hall.

She slunk further back into the shadow of one of the elevated walkways that connected the buildings, chastising herself for being complacent. The empty city had dulled her vigilance. She hadn't seen them approaching the building and could only hope they hadn't seen her either.

"Pull it together, Mace," she whispered to herself.

When the door closed behind them, she waited for her breathing to slow before dashing across the street.

The school was an older building with smaller half-windows so Macie was able to sit flush against the wall beneath the window frame.

"Citrone marks a step to the right, Citrone marks a step to the right, Citrone marks a step to the right, take a breath and beware."

After a few minutes of steeling her nerves and listening for approaching footsteps, Macie popped her head up and took a quick look inside. She had to know if she had been seen; if they were reporting her. Motes were not the only form of city surveillance.

At first, it was just a glance and retreat. Then—

more confident she hadn't been spotted—she took a longer gaze through the glass. Scores of numan youths were in a large room studying eduguides at small desks arranged in a rigid grid pattern.

An instructor sat at a larger desk with his eyes closed—his mind likely lost to the BigDry. Behind him, a large screen repeated a short loop of Wolfram mouthing something over and over. He sat on a high-backed chair surrounded by exploding fireworks. As the sparks of each explosion diminished, the words Happy Upgrade Day flashed above his head.

For five minutes she stood at the window, mesmerised by the stillness of the students. None of the youths moved from their desks nor broke their attention to their studies. School was certainly not the stimulating environment she had imagined.

Satisfied all numankind were too busy to notice one rogue human, Macie left the school buildings and moved on to her real goal.

***

"Should you be here?"

The darkness of the library's old stone foyer made it difficult for Macie to see the owner of the voice that echoed through the empty building. A dark body shape was all that was visible against the blinding sunlight outside. It reminded her of the shadow in the water, although—as her eyes adjusted to the light—the shape resolved into a person, not a watery mirage.

"Aaron." She breathed with an audible sigh of relief. Too much time spent in her own thoughts, she reasoned.

"I saw you walking past the study hall window. What are you doing on this side of the city? Is there a problem with the wall?"

"No. No problem." Macie pulled at her hair, struggling to find the words to explain herself.

"Well," he said in a voice that was all too much like his father's.

"It's just that—" Macie looked around, searching for an excuse.

"Studying up on wall history?" he said, nodding in a way that led her to say more.

"Yes, yes that's it. Whenever I'm not patrolling or repairing, I pop in here for a spot of research."

"Don't let me keep you."

She lifted her foot to move, realising mid-step she didn't know which way to go.

On her only other visit, Roy had taken her to see pictures of animals that had once roamed the land; dingoes, koalas, and Tassie devils. They had viewed the animals via a public access eduguide. Now she needed to look like she frequented the engineering eduguides.

Where Vala, where?

Macie flicked her eyes up at the eagle's ribbon.

"What do those words mean?" she asked, buying time.

"Knowledge, Technology, Efficiency."

Macie leaned sideways to look beyond the foyer into the rows of ancient books with real paper inserts and leather-bound covers.

Aaron turned to follow her eyes.

"You haven't been sourcing your materials through books, have you? So inefficient."

Her downcast eyes told a story of ignorance no numan could ever truly understand.

"I forgot. You wouldn't have gone to school, would you? Sorry. Come on, I'll show you." Aaron grabbed her by her backpack and led her over to the nearest counter.

"Eduguides 101," he said with a crinkled lip that might have indicated a numan attempt at humour. He slid open a panel on the desk and picked up a small solid object, just like the one Macie had seen on her last visit with Roy.

"This little red object is an eduguide cube. It's not really a cube as it has twenty faces. Don't know why it was called that. I do know it holds about one hundred of your human books. There are twenty knowledge centres in the library, each with their own set of eduguide cubes. You just pop it in one of these readers to access the content. Here. Look."

Aaron dropped the cube in a round hand-held device with a series of grey buttons running around its edges. He pressed a button with an arrow icon and a list projected out of the reader onto the white desktop. "Because we are at the information desk, this eduguide is actually about the library. Where you find collections, where the cubes are located, etc."

Aaron scrolled for a few minutes pointing out lists and locations of interest. At times the words flashed past so fast, Macie couldn't even read them.

"Wow, that's a lot of words in such a small object."

"Actually, it's not as impressive as it could be. I did a history project last year. Before The Rise, they could fit a whole library in a device not much bigger than this and it floated in the clouds. Can't figure out how they could access it up there, though."

Aaron seemed to be pointing at the roof. Macie followed his finger to the ornate library ceiling and nodded like she understood.

"Anyway, when the waters rose and power was

lost, the ancients' technology was useless. It's probably still up there in the sky somewhere.

"When this city was built, they scrambled to save the old form books and when they established a new power source, the books were copied over onto cubes. I'm sure we could do just as well as the ancients if we had the will. Only a few people ever come here once they graduate. If it's not in the Dry they don't seem to be interested."

Aaron straightened up and touched his port.

"The Dry . . . I just remembered, I have to go back. I need to be back in class before my teacher comes out of the upgrade."

"Why's it taking so long? The last upgrade was over in a few minutes—this has been going on for hours. There aren't even any motes around. The streets are deserted."

Aaron shrugged. "Won't know till it's over. Which could be any minute. Got to go."

"I should go too. If the upgrade's over then I need to be back on the wall." Macie picked up her bag and started to walk out.

"Wait. You stay here and get what you need. I'll come back once school's finished and walk you home. I can be your excuse—wall project research, you know?"

When Macie hesitated, Aaron continued.

"Look, I feel bad about the whole black mote idea. Let me do you this favour, please?"

Macie nodded, wondering whether she was making a big mistake. Still, she had to work out what Vala and Kin both wanted her to discover.

"Right, see you after class. Engineering is that way." Aaron pointed to the left corridor and hurried out of the foyer. Once he was out of sight, Macie pocketed the reader and sprinted down the corridor to the right.

CHAPTER TWELVE:

THE TELLER'S STORY

Citizen records extract.

Citizen	241039a3 "Roy"
DOB	Upgrade 16.27
Class	Human—Incompatible class G23
Occupation	Wall Manager
Spouse	241085b2 "Vala"
Offspring	255200n5 "Ane" Incompatible reclaimed at 13 days
	256103d2 "Derak" Incompatible class G23 missing
Current status	Reclaimed classification—seniority attained.

Citizen	256103d2 "Derak"
DOB	Upgrade 18.36
Class	Human—Incompatible class G23
Occupation	Wall Manager
Spouse	256967d1 "Else"
Offspring	257095a6 "Macie" Incompatible class G23
	257200n5 "Brad" Incompatible reclaimed at birth
Current status	Missing.

. . .

Citizen	256967d1 "Else"
DOB	Upgrade 18.98
Class	Numan—class A0
Occupation	Urban Planner. High Councillor.
Spouse	256103d2 "Derak"
Offspring	257095a6 "Macie" Incompatible class G23
	257200n5 "Brad" Incompatible reclaimed at birth
Current status	Amalgamated.

Macie turned off the cube's projection and sat back in her chair. It was a shock to finally learn her parents' names, something Vala had never revealed. *Unnecessary* was her standard response to family questions until, during one particularly heated pre-teen interrogation, Macie had caught her with tears in her eyes and let the matter drop.

My mother's status is amalgamated?

Her father Derak was missing, her brother Brad had been reclaimed at birth and there were so many G23s in her family. She turned the reader back on and searched for classification keys for an explanation.

Medical disorder classification extract.

Genetic disorder class G21	Williams syndrome
Genetic disorder class G22	Asperger syndrome
Genetic disorder class G23	Emoto-colorum synaesthesia syndrome

---

A crashing noise in a far off section of the library drew Macie's interest. She stood up and tried to locate its source. Seeing only a curious jade dust rising in the distance, she resisted the temptation to investigate. It was most probably a careless student knocking over a stack, and if school was out, that meant the upgrade was finished.

Hurry, Mace, she thought to herself as she fumbled to activate another cube.

The sounds grew louder. The dust had reached her position. The air was shifting to a deep, nervous green.

"Don't panic, keep reading," she muttered aloud as she scrolled through the entries in a medical classification cube.

> Emoto-colorum synaesthesia syndrome.
>
> Inheritable brain disorder whereby abnormally dense cortex structure causes a sensory perception disorder. Common symptoms include; words being experienced as physical sensations on the skin, sounds experienced as tastes, or emotions experienced as colours.
>
> All forms of synaesthesia render the brain incompatible with cortical implants.
>
> Recommended treatment: Reclamation.

"MACIE!"

She stood to look over the stacks. Aaron was running towards her from the direction of the noise which was growing louder every moment. He was waving his hands as he yelled. All around him, the jade cloud of concern intensified.

"Crap," said Macie. She pocketed the reader and grabbed a handful of cubes, then bolted three stacks over to a section which she hoped shelved a more appropriate subject matter for a Wall Manager. She perched on a stool at a reader and popped in the nearest eduguide.

"Hello, Aaron," she said, without looking up when he reached her position. Macie tried to look casual as she continued a steady rhythm of viewing and discarding cubes. Aaron was panting.

"You numans ought to exercise more."

"Didn't you hear me yelling?"

Out of the general hubbub came an ear-piercing grinding noise which made him flinch.

"Were you yelling? Sorry, I was absorbed in these fascinating books."

Aaron, still puffing, picked up one of the cubes of the desk.

"Japanese water painting of the Muromachi Period?" he said, between heavy breaths.

"Yes. I think I will . . . redecorate the workshop. A few paintings of sunsets might cheer things up. Maybe a dash of pink," she said, miming herself painting pictures.

"Whatever. We have to go." Aaron grabbed her arm and half lifted her off the stool.

"Just one more, I'm sure the wall is fine," said Macie, deliberately misunderstanding him, acting as though she was deep in study. "If you are worried, you can send one of your black motes to check."

"Look!"

Aaron slapped the cube out of her fingers and

physically turned her head to face the noise. It took a moment for Macie to finally register what was alarming him.

"I know," he said, seemingly referring to the library commotion, but the source of Macie's distress was much more personal. She was having trouble getting past his warm hands on her cool cheeks. Vala was the only person to have touched her since she was a child.

She had to bite the inside of her lip to help her focus until he moved his hands. Only then could she collect herself enough to lean forward and squint through the growing dust cloud.

The commotion at the far end of the library had now reached the mid-point, and the cause was becoming clear. Hundreds of black motes were using their new articulated arms to rip apart the library.

Shredded fragments of ancient books and splinters of shattered cubes littered the air. Everything the motes touched was broken or dismantled and thrown into the gaping mechanical mouths of the large demolition motes. Behind them, massive construction motes rumbled in, punching through pillars.

In the distance, the ceiling began to fall. Shafts of light dropped in through the tears but the motes, intent on total destruction, did not stop.

A cracking noise as loud as thunder reverberated

all around them and a gash appeared in the ceiling directly above. Plaster tumbled down onto the desk.

Macie fell backwards. Aaron pulled her back up. "Come on!"

CHAPTER THIRTEEN:
UPGRADE TO THE PAST

Macie stopped running just outside the foyer. Their path was blocked. All the way down Mauve 3, buildings were being demolished.

"The schools! Are there kids still inside?"

Aaron looked sick and seemed to struggle with his response. "Not really. The upgrade's over. Look, it's complicated—I'll tell you later. We have to get out of the school district."

The library steps quaked beneath their feet as though the earth itself were ripping apart. The façade of the once treasured building shook and the lights above them swayed.

"This way," shouted Aaron, leaping down the steps two at a time. Macie followed, and as she reached the ground, an explosion of stone debris burst from the library, sending her hurtling forward onto the paved road.

She pushed herself up and looked back. The great eagle had fallen where they were standing only seconds earlier.

"Are you all right?" Aaron helped Macie to her feet. She nodded her head, although her eyes were wide and she caught her hands trembling.

"What's going on!" she demanded, coughing up demolition dust as she stooped to retrieve her bag.

Aaron paced back and forth, wringing his hands, as if searching for something. A way out perhaps.

"Clearly we can't go down Mauve," Macie said. "Let's try this way."

A black mote sped over to them, waving a cutting tool aggressively with one of its articulated arms. Macie picked up a chunk of what had been the eagle and dropped it firmly on the mote's back, smashing it to pieces.

"What's going on?" Macie yelled.

Aaron looked as though he was going to say something, when a new crashing noise from the distance changed his mind. He took off at a fast pace.

Macie followed him around the corner of the

crumbling library and down the first lane to the right, Kohl-3. They were moving parallel to Mauve, along the backs of classrooms which were yet to be touched by the motes.

Aaron stopped to catch his breath, giving Macie a moment to investigate. She approached one of the large school windows.

"I wish you wouldn't. Please, Macie." A wide-eyed Aaron backed away, hand clenched over his mouth.

The sun was making its trek towards the horizon and its reflection was bouncing off the glass. She had to go right up to the pane and cup her hands around her eyes to see inside. Then she understood Aaron's reluctance.

It was the classroom she had peeked into from the other side on her way to the library. Aaron's classroom, where he had sat amongst twenty-something students only hours earlier. Where their teacher had stared blankly during the upgrade and Wolfram's image had beamed. Only now, everything was darker.

The teacher's body was slumped motionless at his desk. The students' bodies were clustered at the front of the class and she could make out leads going from their cranial implant ports to the big screen at the front of the room. No one was moving.

"What? They… they look like they're dead," she

said, backing away from the window.

"Yes, kind of. It's complicated."

 "What's going on?"

Aaron looked down at his feet.

"Speak to me! What's happening?" she said resisting the urge to shake an answer out of him.

"It's the upgrade. Something went wrong."

A large demolition mote wheeled around the corner of the street, casting distorted shadows and moving menacingly towards them. As it rumbled down the street, it extended an arm with a heavy scoop which it used to smash through the facia of each building it passed. In its wake, a swarm of black motes entered the street to collect the debris.

"We need to get off the streets." Aaron took off at a fast pace. Turning another corner, they split up and tried to open each door they passed without success. Moving swiftly down three roads, they tested dozens more. All locked.

"Damn electronic doors," he said.

Then Macie spotted an older building and guessed it might have an old-fashioned mechanical lock. Sure enough, three paved steps led down to a sub-basement door with a real door knob. The bottom step was caked in dirt, as though few people or motes ever moved over the threshold. It appeared to be as neglected and forgotten as her own workshop.

She turned the knob and gave the door a push. Nothing.

"Here, give me a hand," she called.

Aaron joined her. They braced their shoulders against the door and together they shoved it open.

Lights activated as soon as Macie stepped inside. It was surprisingly chilly and Macie inhaled deeply. The air had a lemony crispness that was a pleasant change after the choking dust outside.

She was about to comment on it, when she realised Aaron was focussed on what was ahead of them. Row after row of banks of technology.

"Whoa!" said Aaron, running his hands over the units as he walked down the closest row. "Do you know where we are?"

Macie shrugged.

"This must be Central Control. I've only ever heard rumours about its existence. This is the autonomous hardware that runs our entire city. This is the BigDry; where it all starts and ends."

Despite his enthusiasm for the contents of the building, Aaron still looked sad. Macie walked over and reached a hand out to his arm.

"What happened with the upgrade? Tell me, Aaron?"

Aaron took a moment to speak, as though searching for the right words.

"We got a summary report when it was over. Apparently, while everyone was upgrading, they had a city-wide debate of a few new council resolutions. That's why it took so long."

"Right . . ." said Macie, trying to draw him out.

"Resolution one; they resolved to end partial implants for older children. No more schools or eduguides needed. Kids over five get adult implants with full citizenship in the Dry."

"Wow," said Macie.

"That's not all. Resolution two; all lower functionaries and aged numans are to be relocated to live in pods in their workplaces to improve efficiency. No more individual homes."

"Poor Gran," said Macie, shaking her head.

Aaron nodded and continued.

"Resolution three; all higher functionaries and compatible children over five are encouraged to amalgamate with the council."

"I don't understand—what is amalgamation?" asked Macie, remembering her mother's record in the library.

"Amalgamation means their personality, knowledge and history are permanently uploaded into the online world and their physical form is reclaimed. It means they will be immortal, in the BigDry."

"Is that why the students were . . ." Macie couldn't bring herself to say the word.

"Yes, dead in the physical world, but very much alive online. Apparently it was contentious. It took some time to get the majority vote, so once it was through they started with the kids to speed up their family's acceptance of the amalgamation. All numans now have three days to either move into their work pods or amalgamate. Superfluous buildings and resources are being reclaimed."

"That's what happened to my mum. It was in her records. I didn't know what it meant until now. I can't believe anyone would choose that."

"I don't. That's why I ran. The time I've spent with you has opened my eyes. I don't want to be a Wall Manager, but I don't want … *that*. So I left as soon as I heard. But they'll catch me eventually. Father can't have the embarrassment of an heir rejecting the grand plan, can he?"

Macie had never seen a numan so close to tears.

"I don't know what to do," he said quietly.

"I do. Come on," she said, heading back into the street.

Aaron rushed to follow her.

"Wait, there is something else you need to know. There was a fourth resolution. One of the biggest arguments against mass amalgamations was relinquishing personal physical freedom."

Macie turned. Her face must have registered confusion as Aaron sighed deeply and rephrased his message.

"The ability to escape flood. You know it wasn't always this way. There are stories of the time before. During The Rise there were explosions in the sky, terrible waves. Famine. War. The horrible exodus from drowning cities.

"They wouldn't accept the resolutions unless certain safeguards were in place."

"Right. And, so?" said Macie.

"Resolution four. Use the material from the reclaimed buildings to construct a bigger, automated wall. No more Wall Managers."

CHAPTER FOURTEEN:
MILK AND COOKIES

My people are changing, I cry for their cooling hearts,
Everyone strives for beige now, blending in has become their art.
The Wolframites march greyly as they storm the galleries,
No progress in aesthetics, is their justifying plea.

Drastic reassignment awaits, for those of us resolved
To keep creativity alive against the ignorance spreading like mould.

Little do they realise, different is gold.

City Artistic Director Wall Manager Raven, Upgrade 17

The sun was low on the horizon by the time they arrived at Vala's apartment block, leaving the city side of the building cloaked in deep aubergine shadows. Macie did a double-take. For the first time, she wondered how much of the colour she saw was due to her bleak emotional state.

Even though the accommodation district was largely untouched by the destructive motes, there was change in the air. It was usually so quiet in the evenings that Macie would have been instantly identified as an outsider who didn't belong. Instead, the streets were flush with numans making last-minute preparations for their own moves; one numan carrying parcels stopped to console another with a very un-numanly hug.

And no motes trailed her. No reason to clean up the DNA of the doomed obsolete.

"Do you remember that time when you accused me of spying for my father? Actually, it was at least three times, come to think of it."

Macie urged her cheeks not to blush in response.

"Well, you were only *mostly* wrong."

"I knew it!"

"No need for fist-pumping. As a nineteen-year-old student, it's true that I've only ever had links to the eduguides, entertainment, memory download and limited messaging. Adults, however, have fully integrated access to everything and in return Wolfram can access their visual and auditory feed.

"With all this upheaval, he probably won't be interested in Vala's feed. Your face, however, might trigger his pre-set recognition programs. You are the only human and your work is still essential to his safety. He's been monitoring you for a long time."

"How do you suggest I speak to Vala then?"

"Well, the first question is whether we really have to visit your grandmother right now. Is this essential?"

"Yes. It could be the last time I see her, and I need to confirm a few things critical to . . . my work."

Aaron rolled his eyes and ran his fingers through his loose hair. It was the first time she'd seen him without his tight plait. He looked almost human.

"And it's important to me."

"All right, just stay out of her line of sight and let me do the talking. What do you want to know?"

***

Aaron rapped his knuckles on Vala's door and Macie took her place to the side of the entrance where she would not be seen.

She looked down the corridor of the soon-to-be-demolished building, noticing the carpet had a peach fleck through it and the lights cast a slightly apricot glow. Strange, when it was her home it had all appeared a predictable grey, like the polished concrete outside. Now the interior looked impermanently pastel.

"Hello, Vala. Apologies for the lateness of the hour."

"That's fine."

"You probably already know my classmates amalgamated today. I'll be doing that myself, soon." He cleared his throat. "I would like to complete my wall project report first, though. It may provide insights relevant to resolution four."

"I'd expect nothing less. Wolfram always has his eye on things. How can I help?" Vala said. Was there a hint of concern in Vala's voice, or was Macie just imagining it?

"There were a few questions your granddaughter was unable, or perhaps unwilling to answer. You know how emotional humans can be. She's always waving her hands around; scared of this, worried about that, watching for conspiracies *around every corner*, taking every precaution she can to *remove herself from spying eyes*. As if anyone need have any secrets from numankind."

Macie smiled when she realised what Aaron was doing. As he performed his mockery of her, he was subtly pointing to her position outside the door and the port on

114

his neck.

Vala dimmed the lights in response. "Yes, I understand. Come in, I was just going offline anyway. I hope you don't mind I have my lights dimmed. All the extra work at the Reclamation Centre has left me with a headache. I do find the dark soothing.

"Perhaps I'll leave the door ajar as well? Let some fresh air in. That way I'll be revived to do my part tomorrow. I'm moving into a lovely new pod at the Reclamation Centre."

Aaron walked into the darkened apartment. Macie waited for a sign to follow them. She heard Vala say, "Do you mind if I sit on my couch to rest my feet?"

"Actually, I might sit there too. I think we can glimpse the last hint of sunset through the window."

Hoping that was her cue, Macie slipped inside and crouched down behind the couch.

"Aaron. You might not be aware, but these walls are quite thin and I'd hate to disturb the neighbours. They are elderly too and likely to be just as exhausted as I. Perhaps we should keep this conversation brief and quiet."

"Agreed. Let's start with your husband, Roy. In his time, he made two significant improvements to the grouting formula. Macie has also performed admirably, for an incompatible. Your son wasn't able to function at the same level though. What happened to him? How is it that some of your family succeed in wall management despite their disability?"

Macie could hear Aaron get up and start pacing. He seemed nervous. It was pleasantly human.

"The disability goes back countless generations on Roy's side of the family. Their minds link colours to their feelings. I think they find numanity difficult, not only because of their incompatibility with technology, but because—to them—we must seem so rigid and colourless.

"They are drawn to the sea because it has all the turmoil and unpredictability that stirs emotions we appear to lack."

"And your son?" prompted Aaron.

"He became obsessed with the idea that the sea was using colour to speak with him. He would say that on the wall he heard his true 'kin' calling him. He took me to see it once. I could only see the shifting tides, nothing else. I think that was the breaking point. No-one knew he had access to a boat until the day he sailed away."

"I don't remember Dad," Macie whispered.

Vala took a moment to continue as though wrestling with rare numan concepts. "Aaron, if you see Macie again, please tell her not to feel too bad if she can't remember him. She was very little at the time. She needs to know he loved her dearly. I'm sure he would have come back to her, if he could.

"It was such a difficult time for everyone. Macie's mother, Else, tried to convince doctors to perform an experimental procedure on little Macie, to cure her. She wanted them to realign Macie's synapses so she was no longer incompatible. She argued it would help Macie have a normal numan life. They denied her request. Inefficient use of resources, I think they said."

"And the Amalgamation?" asked Aaron.

"Yes, Else was one of the first to accept amalgamation. At the time it was as experimental as Macie's surgery.

"I remember her telling me that once she was an amalgamated councillor, she would have greater power. She was confident she could reverse the surgery decision."

"What happened?" Aaron's footsteps slowed and his voice dropped.

"Unfortunately, they didn't have the tech quite right. Wolfram went first, then when Else amalgamated a few days later, his personality was too dominant, I guess—he totally absorbed her. She disappeared. Occasionally, I think I catch shadows of her in the BigDry. She was as beautiful as Macie, you know."

117

"That's . . . hang on, my father has just connected with me."

He sat on the couch. For the longest time, the apartment was silent, broken only by the distant noise of demolition motes and the restless ocean.

"Sorry about the interruption, Vala. I must go now. Given that my teachers are no longer available, Father concluded my wall project prematurely. Now he insists I have no reason to be here. I am to prepare for amalgamation tomorrow." Aaron stood to leave.

"Thank you for your time and for the view," he said, moving back to the window.

Macie took a risk and peeked around the edge of the couch. Vala leaned over a little and extended her hand backwards. Anyone watching would have assumed she was scratching an itch on her back, not caressing the shoulder of her beloved granddaughter.

"No, thank you for coming. I'll miss our conversations."

CHAPTER FIFTEEN: SHIFTING TIDES

His name was Li-Kwan, though he doesn't exist in city records any more.

His home has been occupied by a young geneticist called Jamie, who claims to have lived there all his life.

Li-Kwan's manager at the construction department denies he was ever transferred there and laughs when I accuse his workers of pushing him off the unfinished ninth floor.

His PhD thesis has disappeared from City Library, his climate-demography works are no longer discussed, and no one cares about his flood survivor theories.

No one asks, anymore, why we are named DarwinTwo instead of DarwinOne.

Li-Kwan did.

Wall Manager Po-Kwan, Upgrade 8

Macie was sorry to see Aaron leave. The more time she spent with him, the more human he appeared. As he said goodbye, she could have sworn she saw concern in his eyes. They were still numan eyes, but as she walked into her workshop, she was sure they hadn't been as black anymore. They were more of a deep navy streaked with gold.

Exhausted and falling back on habit, she packed her repair bag and went straight back outside. He was still there.

"Aaron?"

"All this time I've spent with you . . ."

He stopped speaking and avoided her eyes. Shuffling his feet and rolling his shoulders, it was as if he was trying to physically accommodate uncomfortable words that needed to be spoken.

"Don't get me wrong, I don't want to spend my life as a Wall Manager, but these past weeks have shown me a different way of existing. Being in the real world like you. Touching people. Seeing the sky. Feeling the wind. I can't spend the rest of my life as a digital memory of my physical form."

He exhaled loudly and looked deep into Macie's eyes as if they might hold a resolution.

"What are you going to do?" she asked.

"I don't know."

"Come on. I have something to show you." Macie led him inside her workshop.

***

"Is that a . . . does that thing move on water?"

"It's called a boat."

Aaron looked confused. For all of his knowledge, a boat was clearly a foreign concept to him.

"A boat is like a mote that travels on the sea. Remember Vala mentioned my father leaving in a boat. We could do that too."

"What?"

"We could go somewhere else. I've been reading an old journal. Others have left, you know. It's not impossible."

Truthfully, Macie was surprised Aaron had allowed himself to be led out to the dock so easily, and was certain he would reject her offer. It had been like herding a sleepwalker, only that had ended when they had approached the water.

"No. Definitely not. Even reclamation would be preferable to that. Are you mad? Travelling on the endless sea?" Aaron backed up a step, shaking his head.

"Aaron. It's just water. You told me yourself that it couldn't really hurt you. Time to get over it!"

It was difficult to see the height of the waves under the cloudy evening sky, but as they spoke, Macie could hear the sea begin to churn. The little boat jiggled against its moorings and the crest of a small wave bumped the underside of the dock, clattering loose boards as it came into shore, spraying brine-laden air at Aaron.

She heard his sharp intake of breath and rummaged quickly through her bag for something to stave off his panic.

"Here, this might help."

She handed him a small torch which he shone down onto his wet shoes. He rubbed each foot in turn on the back of his pant legs. The action distracted him enough to calm his breathing, while Macie searched for her own courage.

Come on Mace what have you got to lose.

The clouds thinned and the gentle glow of moonlight bathed the dock. The wall next to Aaron glistened iridescently. That last wave had to have been Kin. All around them, the chop of the sea was intensifying.

"Aaron, there's something else I need to tell you."

Another wave charged towards the dock, only this time it was large enough to breach the wooden safety railing.

"Aaron, climb the ladder. Watch from the wall."

She turned back to the wave, holding out a raised palm.

"No, Kin!"

The wave continued rolling in, and as it moved up the shallow shore under the dock, its crest grew. It flowed swiftly over the dock and rose to a height at least twice as tall as Macie. She held one hand up in a feeble attempt at a stop signal, and the other waved the shocked Aaron towards the wall.

"Climb, Aaron. Climb!"

As the roaring wave closed in on her, she shut her eyes and steeled herself. Maybe this wave wasn't Kin. Maybe this was just a normal wave and it was going to pick her up and slam her against—

Nothing happened.

Macie unclenched one eye, then the other. In front of her, a continually churning water wall bent around her form in a half-cylinder, with froth bubbling at the ends like a petulant child trying to reach around its mother.

Understanding it would not hurt her, Macie reached her hand the last short distance to make contact. Immediately, a flash of scarlet hostility scorched her mind. Kin's voice bellowed through her brain.

Enemy! Danger! Abomination is near.

"No Kin. Friend."

Wrong Macie! He carries the abomination which enslaves mankind. It turned them away from nature and devastated the planet. Now it tricks them into ignorant slumber. This is not Emoto's way. His kind must not live.

The water pushed against her hand with a force that belied its liquid form. Macie leaned into it with equal force, still, she slid backwards a few steps.

"Wait, Kin. No! Aaron is friend."

It fools you. He reeks of the technology that ruined this world. Through the centuries, Emoto's followers have taught us, concentrated our sentience and turned us into a life-force that can cleanse the Earth of this foul abomination.

"What do you mean? What is Emoto?"

Kin is the manifestation of Emoto's original discovery of water's aptitude for storing emotions. Kin is his promise of a world lived in harmony through intelligent water. Technology is the problem, we are his ancient solution.

Kin pushed harder. Her feet slid a few steps closer to the wall.

"Aaron, I can't hold it. I'm sorry, you must go!" she yelled.

Too late. Kin had resumed its natural form and washed around her to collide with the wall. Kin's spray reached high into the sky and fell over the wall onto the workshop's rooftop just as Aaron's foot disappeared over the ladder.

Macie bent over and clutched at her knees, catching up on the breaths she had forgotten to take. She crouched down in what was left of Kin as it washed back down the dock on a path to the sea, trying desperately to re-establish communication with her hands.

"I don't know what to do for him, for all of them," she sobbed.

As the last of the iridescent water trickled through her fingertips, the only sound was the clang of her boat against the dock and Kin's parting message which echoed in her heart.

Open the city. Let us fulfil Emoto's promise.

CHAPTER SIXTEEN: DEADLINED

There is nothing heavier than a pen when difficult news needs to be written.

Last night, the comms station outside my workshop rang. Such a rare event, it would have awakened me had I not already been tossing and turning on my cot.

It was City Accommodation Manager Anderson. He informed me that my services are no longer required and my workshop will be demolished to make room for the new wall. I have 24 hours to report for reclamation.

Now Aaron is unable to move forward. Vala is unable to stay put. I am unable to move back. The only solution is more dire than I ever thought possible, and yet inaction will mean the end.

Wall Manager Macie, Upgrade 24

A sleep-deprived Macie stepped out of the workshop to do her usual morning perimeter check.

"Let's go," she said, but the grey mote wasn't waiting at her feet. Instead, there were many motes, all black, and all scuttling over the building opposite her. She blinked the sleep out of her eyes, shook her head, then turned around and went straight back inside.

Slapping her cheeks awake, she tipped the repair items out of her backpack and replaced them with anything precious within arm's reach. The journal, a holopic of young Vala, a multi-tool, some nutri-blocks and a bottle of water.

The stone cross drew her attention. She picked it up, felt the weight of it, and was wondering whether it would slow her down, when there was a firm knock at the door.

For a moment, she considered ignoring it. The motes could begin demolishing the workshop at any time. She had to salvage what she could, no time for visitors.

A second knock piqued her interest.

"What now?"

It was Aaron looking sheepish in the alleyway. Macie shut the door firmly in his face and went back to scavenging in the secret back room. Aaron walked in anyway.

"No. You do not get to come into my home uninvited, even if it is just a crappy old workshop that's about to be demolished. Get out!"

"I'm sorry, I never intended for any of this to happen."

Macie ignored him and surveyed the shelves for more treasures that would fit in her bag; a burgundy purse, a plastic apple, a rusted red harmonica . . .

"Talk to me!" he said, pulling the harmonica out of her hand and slapping it back on the shelf.

"What do you want me to say, Aaron?" she said, and without looking up, she continued her fossicking. A little toy firetruck, a necklace made of coral . . .

"You have to believe me, I had no idea."

"Right."

"Seriously! I was just lodging my report. I had no idea they would use it to justify replacing you with black motes."

"What did you think was going to happen, Aaron? You showed Daddy Wolfram a way to replace me and he did. Now I'm being reclaimed. Another pesky human gone." Macie mimed washing her hands as she finished her rant.

"He wouldn't see it that way. Wolfram is just looking after the best interests of the city."

"That's so numan," she spat the words through

gritted teeth.

"You say that like it's an insult."

"It is!"

Macie pushed past him and went through the workshop, out onto the street.

"Wait," Aaron said, racing to catch up. "Where are you going?"

"To be honest, I'm not sure."

There was a clatter and they both looked up. A black mote was clambering over the roof of the workshop.

"Hey, get down from my roof." Macie rummaged in her backpack, found the multi-tool and hurled it through the air, catching the mote by surprise. It fell to the street with a satisfying crunch. Macie kicked it at a construction mote that had rolled into the alleyway.

"Get your crap away from my workshop!" she yelled, despite knowing it would make no difference. Aaron tried to pull her back. She shook him free.

"I can fix this," he said.

"No, you can't."

Macie climbed onto the construction mote, yelling a stream of hostilities at all motes, Aaron, Wolfram and numankind in general. A black mote crawled aggressively towards her, waving its arms as though trying to rid itself of a buzzing fly. She grabbed hold and smashed it on the road below.

"Hang on."

Aaron picked up the broken mote and stopped talking as his eyes glazed over. Macie could see his Adam's apple moving, a clear sign of sub-vocalising. She didn't care. She had nothing left to lose. She climbed further up the construction mote and bashed it with all her strength. Surprisingly, it stopped and the smaller motes withdrew.

"Come down," Aaron said, offering his hand.

"Well that worked. Mote cowards!" she shouted at her metal nemesis, before jumping down without accepting Aaron's help. She made a show of dusting off her hands.

"I spoke to Dad."

"Look, I don't need your—"

"I pleaded your case. Reminded him that we had a duty of care to keep you safe until your reclamation."

"Right. And that worked?"

"No. So I showed him this broken mote and suggested the auto repair system might need some expert tweaking. It'll take them a day or two to review the programming. They need you to keep managing the wall in the interim. They've moved your reclamation to tomorrow."

"Oh gee, a few more hours. Helpful."

"Look, Mace. You're not the only one being reclaimed. I went past the Reclamation Centre on the way here. There are hundreds of numans volunteering for reclamation rather than amalgamation into the BigDry or relocation into workplace pods."

Macie mulled this over for a moment. "Show me."

***

Walking freely through the city, bereft of corralling motes, was an unnatural experience for Macie. She would have enjoyed it, had there not been such urgency to their mission—whatever that mission may be. Whatever she decided to do, it had to be done soon, before . . . She pushed the thought away. The word 'reclamation' left a bitter colour in her mouth.

Delivery motes and numans carrying relocation bags were everywhere. Two big demolition motes growled in the distance. It would only take a few weeks and the city would be unrecognisable.

When they drew closer to the Reclamation Centre, Macie could smell the sickening odour of resolution one. There was a queue of numans with downcast eyes and low-hung heads going in one side of the building. On the other side, carriage motes queued up to remove the output of raw materials.

"What do you have in mind?" asked Aaron, stopping to run his fingers through his loose hair.

"Come on."

Macie moved through the crowd to the door she had used to secretly visit Vala. She rapped on the metal and whistled her old wispy signal.

"When Vala comes out, tell her to find a way to shut down the Centre for a few hours," Macie said.

"How's she going to do that?"

"Don't worry, she's resourceful. Then make sure she gets back to her apartment and stays there. It's on the fourth floor, that should be safe."

"And what are you going to do?"

"You don't want to know."

"Well, what about the rest of these people?"

Macie looked around at the never-ending queue of numans. "Is there any way we can speak to them without Wolfram knowing?"

"You and I can't, but Pete might." Aaron pointed to an adolescent further back in the queue. He looked just like Aaron, only not quite as tall.

"How did he skip student amalgamation?"

"Pete has a minor learning challenge and only just escaped reclamation as a child. He was the only student in our class not to receive the offer of amalgamation."

"Lucky Pete," said Macie.

Aaron raised his eyebrows. "Yeah, lucky Pete—he gets reclamation instead."

Macie didn't know what to say. Numans had always seemed so unfeeling, but Aaron was genuinely upset about what was happening. They all were. And yet, in true numan fashion, they all continued to follow orders.

"Anyway," continued Aaron, "Pete's known to be an under-achiever, so Wolfram wouldn't bother monitoring his feed. Plus, when Vala logs him as arrived at reclamation, all his circuits will go offline. He'll be no more connected to the Dry than you are."

"Can we rely on him to help?"

"Absolutely, he hates numankind almost as much as you do."

"Not possible."

"He had a baby sister. Her name was Emily."

Macie clutched her chest at the name. She looked down the dark line of numans awaiting processing. Too many faces tinged with yellow resolve.

"Right. Speak to Vala, get her to log in as many people as she can before she has her 'accident', then introduce me to Pete. Time to clean up your father's mess."

CHAPTER SEVENTEEN:
THE CLEANSE

Yesterday, Vala asked me outright whether I was talking to the water like our son Derak did. I lied. Never lied to her before. Feeling lousy about it. First time in all our married years, you know.

I can't trust her any more. You can't trust any of 'em. Since the last upgrade, it's like you tell one of 'em and everyone knows.

Besides, I wouldn't really call it talking. I just go down to the secret dock and call out 'Derak'. Sometimes nothing happens. Sometimes the water rises up to greet me. It feels like it's trying to console me, like it understands my heartache. I cry. It churns. Together we mourn.

Yesterday it was a year since he left and I'm not ashamed to say I howled like a wild storm. I miss him real bad. The sea must have understood as it rose up and slammed into the wall so hard I thought it might breach. I actually yelled out to it, 'Stop you'll break the wall,' and I swear it said "Yesyesyesyes!"

Wall Manager Roy, Upgrade 20

By the time Aaron returned, Macie had made considerable progress on her plan. For two hours, she had been dissolving and chipping away at the mortar between the stones that made up the back wall of the workshop. Already, small trickles were starting to appear, sliding across her hands, flashing tangerine messages of encouragement.

"Macie?"

Aaron was hard to see in the doorway. It was a warm day and strong sunlight was streaming through the door behind him, casting a shadow on his face. His body language seemed more relaxed than normal. Less Wolfram. More human.

"Glad you're back, I could use a hand," she said, wiping sweat from her brow and stretching her back, sore from bending.

"It's not just me," he said, moving aside to allow another shadow into the room.

"Hello, sweetheart," said an unmistakable voice.

"Gran? Oh, Gran!" Macie jumped up to embrace the old woman, half laughing and half crying. "How is this possible?"

"Simple. I logged myself into the Reclamation Centre as a self-punishment for the awful mistake I made, and they locked me out of the BigDry. Ta-da. Without that uplink, you could say I'm basically human again."

"What did you do?"

"I accidentally dropped some nitric acid into the main furnace; they're going to have to shut the whole area down for the rest of the day while hazmat motes scrub it.

"Pity, just before it shut down I logged in the 232 numans who were queued up outside the Reclamation Centre. Now they're all out of the Dry as well now. Wolfram's going to have a devil of a time tracking them all down. Serve him right."

Macie giggled.

Aaron shook his head and held onto the bench beside him.

"Oh, I am sorry love—I forgot he is also your father," said Vala, placing a grandmotherly arm across his stooped shoulders.

"It's all right, we've never been very close. It's just all happening so fast. Two days ago I was planning on graduating and joining the numan ranks. Now my only choice is—"

"Aaron, the right choice is rarely easy. I've lived most of my life hooked into the Dry. At first, it's astonishing—there are more virtual worlds than you can possibly imagine. Science, art, entertainment—there are infinite ways to get lost. Then you go offline and everything looks duller and harder so all you want to do is go back. It's very addictive."

"What am I doing out here then?" he said, in a flat voice.

"Saving yourself from amalgamation," said Vala, sounding weary. "That's the real problem. In an artificial world where you can look and live in any way you can imagine, it's easy to lose track of your true self. You forget who you are. You miss out on the beauty and unpredictability of real life.

"And once you amalgamate, there's no hope. That's how I lost Macie's mother. She thought she could have a greater influence over city policies if she committed everything she had to the BigDry, but as soon as she amalgamated, she was gone.

"It was like her personality was swallowed up by a mash of numankind; no one part distinguishable from the others. That's why Wolfram wants everyone amalgamated. It will give him ultimate control. No individual voices to disagree."

Vala reached out her hand to Macie. "She did it to give you a better life; to save you from reclamation. After amalgamation, she couldn't even save herself."

Vala stopped talking and wiped her eyes. She looked at her fingertips and shook her head. "Can't remember the last time . . . the BigDry was always a good cure for heartache."

Macie opened her mouth, but Vala shushed her and continued speaking.

"I'm all right, love. Let's save the rest of the numans, shall we? What's your grand plan?"

***

Macie held her grandmother's hand as they stood on the little dock and surveyed the ocean. It was surprisingly quiet for all the plans they had made. She had expected to see it all wildly dangerous and raring to go.

"So this is what it looks like."

"You've never seen the ocean, Gran?"

"Not this close. I've seen it from windows and of course Roy tried to get me onto the wall. No, the vastness of it always unnerved me. Especially after your father . . ."

Macie gave her hand a little squeeze. Vala looked behind her to Aaron, who was backed up against the wall,

then whispered into Macie's ear.

"What's with the kid? He's lookin' a little green, even for a numan. It's like he can't decide if he's going to faint or puke."

"He had a bit of a fright last time I brought him down here. Come on, let's get on with this before the motes figure out we're up to something."

Macie walked the short distance back to the wall behind Aaron and checked the grouting. It was almost entirely dissolved at the waterline, and higher up it was missing altogether, showing streaks of light bursting between the stones.

She picked up the crowbar they'd brought and climbed up the rusty ladder. Prying the tool between two stones at the top of the wall, she applied all her strength. At first, nothing happened, so she shifted her weight to give her more power. It lifted a little, not enough.

"Come on, Mace. What would Grandpa Roy say at that feeble attempt? Give it a bit of grunt."

She smiled at Vala who was glowing golden in the bright sun. She'd forgotten how feisty her grandmother could be.

Macie hooked the crowbar under her arms and made a show of stretching her muscles, then she spat in her hands for grip.

"That a girl. Really go for it this time!" yelled

Vala.

Macie wedged the bar back in between the rocks, took one look back at Vala, and then stepped off the ladder. With her full weight working the lever, the old stone gave way, flipping over the wall and onto the workshop roof.

Macie fell back onto the dock, the crowbar landing next to her and rolling over the side into the water.

"No!" cried Aaron, seemingly forgetting his fear and making a late dash for the tool. He stopped at the edge and watched it sink below.

"Are you all right, dear?" said Vala, rushing to Macie's aid.

"Absolutely. Now we know two things. Aaron's almost over his fear of water and this wall is ready to go!"

"Excellent. Aaron, did you get your end of things organised?" asked Vala, as she helped Macie to her feet.

"Um, yes," he said, backing away from the water. "Pete's crew got all the doors of the central control building opened and blocked with furniture so they'll stay that way.

"They tried to pull the covers off the individual processing units too. I asked him to stop that. If they accidentally short something out, Wolfram will send in motes to investigate and that will end all our plans.

Instead, I sent him off to get as many people as possible up to the higher floors and barricade ground floor doors where they can. They should be ready to go."

"Right, then I might ask you both to get in the boat."

"What?"

Macie moved closer to Aaron and tried to give him her most trustworthy look.

"You know we have to do this, Aaron. It's going to get real wet soon. The boat is the only way I can ensure you and Vala are safe."

Aaron nodded and gingerly stepped off the dock, into the old wooden craft.

"You too, Gran."

Vala grinned, hugged Macie and stepped aboard. "Your parents would be so proud of you, sweetheart."

***

Macie watched Aaron row a short distance from the dock. Vala waved, and in her head, Macie pictured a rosy alternative reality where she would join them on board and together they would sail away from the city, leaving the numans to their digital fate. Perhaps they would find her father safe on some distant island.

The boat slowed down into a holding position

and Vala signalled Macie onwards with a nod. It was time.

Macie walked to the end of the dock and looked out at the sea, realising she wasn't actually sure how to start the process. Every time she had talked to Kin, Kin had initiated contact.

She held her hands out over the water and closed her eyes, visualising her watery friend. The ocean was quiet. She called out Kin's name, but the wind blew it back in her face and the sea remained calm.

She turned, looked at Vala and shrugged. Her grandmother nodded encouragement, saying something incomprehensible in the light breeze. Macie waved as though she understood and turned back to the water, grateful no one could see her cheeks blush with embarrassment and frustration. She hadn't expected it to be this hard.

Swaying a little and ramping up into a gig, she stomped her feet on the dock, hoping the vibrations would stir the water spirit. Not even a spritz.

She lay down on edge of the wooden planks and trailed her fingers through the water. Still nothing. The horizon was alarmingly calm.

In a last act of desperation, she rolled over the edge and slid down into the blue liquid.

CHAPTER EIGHTEEN: SEA LEGS

My wife gave me a little book of sea quotes to mark my five year work anniversary. Her way of cheering me up I guess. It's a dreary job at best.

I keep the book in my pocket and pull it out when things grow calm. This one, in particular, takes my fancy:

"What would an ocean be without a monster lurking in the dark? It would be like sleep without dreams." —Werner Herzog

Wall Manager Jergen, Upgrade 3

Making a fundamental miscalculation on land is unfortunate. But, as Macie bobbed just below the surface, she appreciated that a fundamental miscalculation at sea could have a far higher cost. She was swiftly running out of air.

"Kin!"

Twice, she had surfaced for a lungful of air and a call to her watery friend.

"Kin, we need you! Come to me, it is time."

Not seeing any sign of Kin, she had dived straight back down. She waved her hands to sweep away the doubt as she pushed lower into the ocean until she reached the floor, where she cried out with all her heart and mind.

The feeling of a ribbon flitting past her ankles drew her attention. A small school of glittering goldfish was darting up and around her limbs, playing a gleeful game of tag in the tides. They swam close to her face, surrounding her, before rushing up to the surface and then back again.

Macie wasn't in the mood for games. She ignored them and stared at the curving wall, searching for an answer.

Where are you, Kin? Is something stopping you?

Lungs aching, mind growing cloudy, she gave up trying to hold her ocean floor position and let go. She relaxed her arms and drifted with the navy currents, not caring anymore. Sleep would be a better friend, solving many problems.

Thud! A heavy object collected her underside and

pushed her upwards, only it didn't have the soft fluid touch of Kin. It felt heavy, more like a large wall stone which made no sense.

She didn't care. Macie was too weary to think. Her mission was over. She'd failed to find Kin. Nothing would be set right after all. It was cold, everything was dimming to black, and she was ready for oblivion. Macie opened her mouth, welcoming the last deep caress of water, when she unexpectedly burst through the surface.

Gasping to wakefulness, she put her hand out to hold onto whatever had saved her. Coughing and gagging, she opened her eyes. She had expected it to be debris—leftovers from the ancients that could still be spotted from time-to-time riding on the currents . . . but her saviour was much more alive than waterlogged debris.

Wondering if she was seeing it right, Macie shook her head and rubbed her eyes. In front of her was a huge animal with dancing black eyes, long eyelashes and rancid breath.

It one of the animals Roy had shown her so many years ago on the library's eduguides. It nudged her face and slapped her back. Macie coughed out some more water and thanked it with hugs, wishing she could remember the name of the generous animal.

Dolphin, came a thought from outside her own

mind. The animal made a series of high-pitched grunts and whistles, then splashed away at high speed.

"Kin?" she coughed.

All around her, the ocean's surface shimmered, and out of a flat sea, a wave suddenly reared up beneath her.

"Oh, Kin!" she cried, relieved and humbled that it had finally heard her call.

We are sorry we are late. Sent word ahead to other wet friends to help. We were home. We are here now. Let's finish the tell.

Floating on Kin's safe currents, Macie relaxed. The sun on her face warmed her blood and the gentle massage of her powerful friend beneath her back buoyed her confidence. She reached out with her hands and imagined her plan to Kin, visualising the new weak points in the wall and the layout of the city streets beyond.

Kin flushed with crimson understanding and surged forward.

Halfway to the wall, Kin changed direction and powered out towards the boat.

"What are you doing? No!"

A startled Aaron frantically tried to row out of the way, inexperience leaving him turning the vessel in useless circles.

"Kin?"

As Kin's wave grew closer, the little boat rocked and tilted precariously. Macie saw Vala increase her grip.

"Kin, careful! They are friends too. We must protect them. All life is precious."

We shall protect, together.

Kin's speed reduced as they moved within speaking distance of Aaron and Vala.

"Don't worry, it will be all right!" Macie yelled to Aaron.

Slowing to a crawl, Kin's wave lifted her into a seated position and deposited her over the edge of the boat. Aaron and Vala were instantly drenched by Kin's actions. Aaron coughed as though the small splash was drowning him.

Vala laughed for the first time in years, her cheeks flush with un-numanly exhilaration. "Well, aren't you a wonder! You were down there so long I was worried we'd lost you," she said, embracing her soggy granddaughter.

"Tell you the truth, the thought crossed my mind too, Gran. Now sit down and hold on—I think this might be a wild ride."

Macie put her hand out and let her fingers drift through the wave that was defying the natural order of the sea to barrel roll continuously by her side. Her heart filled with the joy of free movement and ecstasy of choice. She knew their actions were right.

"Let's go free them, Kin."

Kin moved off and positioned itself closer to the city, at the edge of the dock. The sky was clear, yet a growling noise slowly approached like the late summer storms from the north. From behind them, and all the way to the horizon, ripples were rising on the surface.

At first it was just a series of white lines pushing the wind ahead of them. Then, as they roared towards the city, the lines merged, peaks formed and a foaming surf rolled under their vessel.

The little boat was buffeted but held stable on the back of the wave. Macie's nose was filled with salty expectation. Aaron gripped his oar tighter. Vala threw her head back and bellowed one of Roy's sea shanties into the wind.

As they merged into Kin the waves powered into a gleaming tsunami holding position at the city wall. It rippled through the spectrum from chartreuse to indigo, then, as though on signal, it folded in on itself and a thoroughly navy Kin thundered up the dock.

The ancient stones were no match for its might. In one wet punch, a gash opened up in the wall and the water flowed through.

"Hold on!" yelled Macie. They were caught in Kin's rip and were sucked towards DarwinTwo, the wave carrying them up and over the crumbled wall. Kin smashed through her workshop and together they streamed into the city streets.

"Yahoo!" cried Vala, who seemed to delight in every pitch and roll.

Macie laughed and sung her navigation song at the top of her lungs. Not that she needed it. Kin's influence was guiding the waters to their target, and—for the first time—she was seeing some of the buildings in full colour.

" . . . Citrone marks a step to the right, take a breath and beware. Amber's world can be busy. Chin up, don't despair." The ladies both laughed and trailed their fingers through the fast-moving water. The boat floated down Jade 3 and careened through the narrow Scarlet 8.

"Gran, it's glorious," Macie hollered over the growling sound of the swell. "I see the colours at last. No wonder you love it!"

Around each corner, the waters surged and small waves broke off to splash up the faces of buildings, alarming the numans who were pressed up against the windows, witnessing the titanic event.

The boat approached an overpass that was not fully enclosed. Macie spied Pete waving his hands and pointing to their approach as he tried to herd two shocked onlookers into an adjoining building.

"Look out!" shrieked Aaron, jumping up and

rocking the boat.

Macie reached out and pulled him back to a seated position, clasping his hand, hoping she had courage for both of them. "Trust Kin."

She closed her eyes and bent over the edge, thrusting her hands deep into the wave. Message apparently received, Kin washed over the bridge and picked up the three ex-numans, placing them gently into the boat.

"Nice of you to join us!" laughed Vala.

"How?" blurted Pete as he looked back and forth between Macie and Aaron. Macie pulled her hands out of the water and shrugged. Pete smiled from ear to ear and reached out to give her a surprisingly human hug.

"Thank you," he said, over and over.

At Amber Road, the street of dread, Kin's wave split in two. One section raced off towards the education district. The other swept them into the city square.

Macie steeled herself, dipping her hand into Kin for reassurance. She tensed, her mood suddenly grey. She poured out her fears to Kin while her other hand gripped Vala's hand.

The abomination is here, Kin told her, and began lapping around the square, keeping the little boat spinning slowly in the middle of a gentle whirlpool. The big screen crackled to life. Wolfram's wide eyes glared down at the boat.

Pity, said Kin.

"Why?" yelled Macie.

Technology consumes. He is beyond cleansing—pity for him. Kin slowed its motion, allowing the wash to splash high up the sides of buildings, right over the top of Wolfram's big screen. When the water drained back, Wolfram looked equal parts shocked and enraged.

"You! And my son. What have you done to him Wall Manager? I can't read him. Have you taken him hostage?"

As he bellowed, the screen flickered briefly. Wolfram looked up as though trying to spot the source of his techno troubles. Then the glitching stopped and his glare focussed on Macie.

"You *can* see me. I knew it!" she said, shaking with anger.

Strength, Kin said, and gave her a shove into a standing position. Vala nodded encouragement, even Pete nodded.

Macie opened her mouth, but her timid words trailed off into the wind.

"Stop mu-mu-muttering and hand over my son!"

The boat bobbed and Macie stumbled.

"Don't let him get to you, Mace," Vala said with a wink.

Macie steadied herself and faced the monolithic smirk.

"I'm not afraid of you," she said quietly.

Wolfram held up his hand in a two-finger salute and laughed.

Images of Vala's bandages ravaged her mind. Without thinking, she clenched her fists, straightened her back and cleared her throat.

"How does it feel to have an 'incompatible' wash away your influence?"

"Really? You're delusional."

"Too long you have enslaved the people of our city. At last, your son has joined me, as have many others, and we say no more!"

Wolfram scoffed. "This is why incompatibles belong in reclamation. Have we not housed and fed you all your life, despite your gross disability? And this is how you repay our numan charity?"

"Disability does not require charity! We have strengths you cannot even imagine."

"Apparently not strong enough to keep your job though?"

Macie dipped her hand back into Kin and was buoyed by an update on their mission.

"I'm not the only one out of a job, Wolfram. The Reclamation Centre has crashed, Central Control is flooded and the wall's down. It's time to swim or drown!" screamed Macie.

The screen flickered and Wolfram's focus drifted.

"What have you done? I'm losing connections—"

The screen went black.

Vala cheered.

"Father—" Aaron rose to his feet.

The boat spun around on an eddy and as she swirled past the screen, Macie thought she might have caught a glimpse of another, softer face before the image of Wolfram's face returned.

He smoothed his hair with his hands, rolled his shoulders, glared and attempted a smile but his twitching upper lip told her all was not calm.

"You know you can't win. Even now, my motes are working to repair your damage."

Movement on a nearby bridge caught Macie's eye. Two black motes were clambering at a fast pace. She assumed they were heading for the wall, but as she watched, they leapt towards her, pincers outstretched. She screamed and the boat spun away on one of Kin's currents, too late. The motes caught the bow and pulled themselves onto the deck.

"Aaron!" Pete yelled, catching one mote and wrestling it to the floor.

"Move back," Macie yelled to Pete, who released

the mote and jumped backwards, just as Macie brought an oar down onto its back. She smashed it in two with just one whack.

The other mote scuttled towards Aaron who was ignoring it, eyes locked on his father's grinning image.

Pete grabbed one leg of the mote as it launched itself at Aaron, causing Aaron to fall forward onto the deck. Pete tugged at the malevolent creature which had a firm hold of Aaron's ankle. He kicked frantically. Macie took aim with the oar, but in the commotion missed and struck the side of the boat instead.

"Let me—" called Vala, joining Pete in the pull. Together, they removed the mote and threw it overboard, where it sunk quickly to the road below. Aaron fell back, panting.

Pete pointed upwards. There were more motes scuttling across the bridge.

"Help us," Aaron pleaded.

"You betray me and now you want my help? Had I known you were this weak, I would have sent you to reclamation years ago. Your kind doesn't deserve immortality," Wolfram's flickering image bellowed. "Dispatch them!"

Hordes of black motes poured down the buildings. Macie concentrated on getting Kin to keep them spinning erratically. It was little help. There were so many motes leaping towards them, it was inevitable that some would connect.

Vala let go of Macie and smacked a mote that was climbing up next to her. Pete picked up the spare oar and pummelled three others.

Macie wasn't sure they could handle too many more. Vala was clutching her chest and breathing heavily as she fought one-handed. She yelled at Aaron to help, but he seemed to be lost in Wolfram's smug face.

"Look at this, Aaron! Danger from water all around us, yet you rejected amalgamation. Why do you think I announced the resolutions? To remove us all from these types of physical dangers. You could have lived safely in the BigDry for eternity."

Aaron sobbed.

"You are too stupid to comprehend that, aren't you? Just a small-minded kid who meddles in that which he cannot possibly understand. How human!" Wolfram bellowed.

Aaron winced, then covered his face with his hands.

A mote leapt directly at Macie's head. The boat rocked violently as she dodged it and scrambled to the back of the boat where it was still mote free.

"You can't win, Wall Manager. Humans will always be inferior!" yelled Wolfram and dozens of black motes cascaded down the sides of his screen.

"Kin, help us." Macie returned her hand to the water and visualised the dark turn of events. She showed Kin the dangerous potential of the boat overturning and the possibility of the motes injuring the newly humanised population.

Abominations! Kin will cleanse this problem.

A second wave barrelled into the square, raising the overall water level and swiping the motes into its wake.

The boat tossed around like a cork. It was all Macie could do to hold on.

Wolfram's face disappeared again, and when it returned to the half-submerged screen, his bulging eyes were bloodshot with rage.

"More waves? How? My motes! Never ... suspected ..." He looked left and right as his image trembled and pixelated. Water continued to slam at the surrounding buildings. Salty spray filled the air. Many motes were swept away.

"My city! Aaron—" cried a distraught Wolfram as his image was completely lost to the rising water. The remaining black motes retracted their limbs and fell into the swell.

"I'm sorry," Aaron said in a small voice.

Vala pulled him onto the seat next to her and

wrapped him in a consoling hug.

"This is not your fault, love. It had to be done. No one person can hold dominion over all. Now Macie, I think it's time to lower the tide."

Macie breathed a calming sigh and sat down. She let her fingers drift into Kin. The waters began to recede.

"Look!" said Vala. All around them, the stunned faces of newly disconnected numans appeared in the wet windows.

The water continued to drop until the boat sat level with the bottom of the big screen. Macie jumped to her feet when it crackled back into life, only this time Wolfram's mug was replaced by that of a woman who looked strangely familiar.

"Else!" cried Vala, letting go of Aaron to stand with her granddaughter. "Sweetie, is that you?"

"Vala?" said the image, its voice catching, soft eyes blinking. "Macie?"

The woman looked tired and much older than Macie had imagined, but the family resemblance was strong. Her mother smiled kindly.

Macie's throat swelled and her eyes stung.

"Thank you, Vala, for raising my girl. I'm so proud of both of you. I don't know how you've done this. It's astonishing. Freedom is all I ever wanted for you, baby—"

Else glanced over her shoulder as though someone was approaching, then the image on the screen dimmed dramatically.

"I've always loved you, Macie," she said gently.

"She's grown up to be an amazing woman, just like you Else. She did all of this," Vala yelled a tumble of rushed words.

"Mum, I—" Macie tried, but it was too late.

Else touched her fingers to her lips as her image froze, then her kiss disappeared.

For the longest time, Macie stood staring at the black screen. Wishing.

EPILOGUE: THE QUIET PROMISE
OF CHERRY BLOSSOM

This will be my last entry. I'm leaving the journal with Aaron as I move forward. He will need this book of advice from the elders to rebuild the city, now there is no automation to serve humans nor BigDry in which to escape.

After Kin withdrew the flood and held the ocean back while we repaired the great gash in the wall, Kin took me and my little boat home to meet Emoto's followers.

On the banks of Mount Fuji where the cherry blossom blooms, I met a humble community of spiritualists and scholars. I walked upon real grass for the first time in my life and ate fresh fruit. I stroked the silver mane of an elderly monkey.

In a temple, by a spring, a priest of knowledge revealed the work they have slaved over for countless generations. Certainly, it goes back to before the great flood. They have expanded upon Emoto's ancient theories of the innate intelligence of water, identifying essential attributes and concentrating the ancient wisdom until eventually Kin was born.

They are indeed a patient and wise people. They have offered to help us rebuild. We are not the only city they have assisted.

The priest was quite old and he remembered my father. He assured me there is always hope.

Tomorrow, I will set sail again. Vala will come with me. She says it's time for another adventure. Together with Kin, we will find Roy. I am hopeful.

Macie, the last Wall Manager.

AFTERWORD

The relationship between Kin and Macie was inspired by the work of Dr Masaru Emoto—a Japanese scientist who postulated that human consciousness could have a physical effect on the molecular structure of water. You can read more about it in his book; *Messages from Water*. It's fascinating stuff, alas his experiments were not able to be replicated by any other scientists. Ultimately, Dr Emoto was discredited.

ABOUT THE AUTHOR

Shel Calopa is a speculative fiction writer from Melbourne, Australia. Shel's published works include *Ruby's Ride* in the *Release of Silence* anthology, *Dugong Dreaming* in the *AQUARIUS* anthology, and a dystopian novel *Letters from the Light*.

Whilst mostly set in the sci-fi genre, Shel's stories only use science as the backdrop. She is more interested in her characters' struggles with contemporary issues of prejudice, ableism, gender politics and the corrupting influence of power.

You can find Shel Calopa on most major socials and read her flash fiction on her website www.shelcalopa.com

ABOUT DEADSET PRESS

Deadset Press is the publishing imprint for Aussie
Speculative Fiction – a community aimed at supporting
Australian and Kiwi authors. You can learn more at:

www.aussiespeculativefiction.com

ABOUT THE SERIES

Drowned Earth is a series of eight standalone novellas, set in a shared world.

Prequel: Shards of Silver by Alanah Andrews
Debbie is on board a ship when an asteroid collides with Antarctica, causing a tsunami. And it's heading her way…
(eBook Only: Free Download)

The Rise by Sue-Ellen Pashley
The great Rise means that resources are scarce and not readily shared. But with her best friend's life at stake, along with some stranded refugees, Katie James knows she must prove there's more to being human than just existing. Even if that puts her on the same kill list.

Fire Over Troubled Water by Nick Marone
Despite winds, torrential rains, storms, and bushfires, a fresh water merchant searches for his lost daughter among the autonomous island communities of flooded eastern New South Wales.

Submerged City by Austin P. Sheehan
Melbourne is under martial law, overseen by general Messinger—an extremist who believes the flood is God's retribution against the left-wing agenda…

Tides of War by Marcus Turner

After discovering a strange man in a row boat, Maria wages war on the lotus cities—clandestine floating communities off the coast of Victoria that are reserved for the wealthy.

The Jindabyne Secret by Jo Hart

With nothing but a map and a rickety solar truck, Jax journeys to the top secret fresh water facility at Lake Jindabyne—one of the few fresh water lakes left in Australia. What he discovers there could be the key to saving his whole community, as long as the government doesn't kill him first.

River of Diamonds by S. M. Isaac

Who would want to leave one of the last idyllic settlements since the Rise? Rosa has a map, a mercenary, and a hope to salvage a future for the world.

Emoto's Promise by Shel Calopa

Five hundred years after the flood, can Macie defeat the technology which has enslaved the last remaining humans in the walled city of Darwin?

Salvaged by C.A. Clark

Cassie lives in the safe haven of academics on the anchored city of new Melbourne. After a diving incident she is rescued by a territorial beach combing gang who trade goods washed up by the frequent storms. Cassie wishes she had never taken her home for granted.

ALSO BY DEADSET PRESS

Annual Anthologies

Beginnings: Australian Speculative Fiction Vol. 1

Journeys: Australian Speculative Fiction Vol. 2

Zodiac Series

Capricorn

Aquarius

Pisces

www.aussiespeculativefiction.com